ONE-WAY TICKET TO THRILLVILLE

Ten Torrid Tales

By

Will "the Thrill" Viharo

ONE-WAY TICKET TO THRILLVILLE

Cover formatting by Dyer Wilk
Interior formatting by Rik Hall – RikHall.com

Front cover photo: Will the Thrill and Monica Tiki Goddess at the Parkway Speakeasy Theater, Oakland, CA., 1998, from the personal collection of the author.

Back cover photo: Monica Tiki Goddess at Forbidden Island Tiki Lounge, Alameda, CA., by Tom Cat Photography for Tiki Oasis, 2010.

Back cover author's photo: Will the Thrill at Forbidden Island Tiki Lounge in Alameda, CA., by Jim Ferreira, 2006.

ISBN-13: 979-8-218-59236-3

First Printing
Printed in the United States of America
Published by Thrillville Press
www.thrillville.net
www.willviharo.com

For David Lynch—

To: WILL
wishing you all the best —
don't stop writing!

CATCHING THE BIG FISH

david lynch

I promise I'll never stop.

"Remember that night in the Garden you came down to my dressing room and you said, 'Kid, this ain't your night. We're going for the price on Wilson.' You remember that? 'This ain't your night.' My *night*! I coulda taken Wilson apart! So what happens? He gets the title shot outdoors on the ballpark and what do I get? A one-way ticket to Palookaville…You don't understand. I coulda had class. I coulda been a contender. I coulda been *somebody*, instead of a bum, which is what I am, let's face it."

—Marlon Brando from a screenplay by Budd Schulberg, *On the Waterfront,* 1954

Table of Contents

NAKED WHORE WITH A GUN

The naked whore had the john's own gun trained on his erect cock.

"Are you going to shoot me?" he asked, standing at the foot of the bed with his pants around his ankles.

"Maybe," she said. "Depends on what mood I'm in."

"Well, what mood *are* you in?" he asked.

"A bad one."

"I guess that doesn't bode too well for me," he said.

"Nope," she said, shaking her head, the motion of which jiggled her bare, banana-shaped breasts. "It sure don't."

"Well, mind if I sit down?"

"Yeah."

"Yeah, I can sit down, or yeah, I mind."

"The second one."

"Meaning no."

"Yes."

"So you *do* mean yes, I can sit down, or - ?"

"I mean *no*. Stand still and shut the fuck up until I say so."

"Okay."

The naked whore took a seat on the bed, with the gun still pointed at the john. His holster was dangling off the bedpost, next to his jacket. Careful not to let him out of her sight, she removed a cigarette from inside the jacket, put it between her lips, and said, "Got a light?"

"Yeah, in my pants."

"I don't mean your dick, asshole."

"Neither do I. My lighter is in my pants pocket. My pants are around my ankles. May I reach down and get it?"

"Sure, just be careful as hell," she said, cocking the piece.

The john reached down carefully, took the lighter out of his pants pocket, and shakily lit her cigarette. She blew the smoke in his face, and he coughed.

"Now, stand back and stay put," she said.

"Sure, for how long?"

"Till I either shoot you or tell you to leave."

"Okay."

With the gun still pointed at the john's crotch, the whore looked around the barren hotel room, then her gaze stopped in the mirror at the bureau. She was fascinated by her own reflection.

"I'm pretty hot, ain't I?" she asked the john rhetorically.

"I think so," he said.

"You like my body?"

"Love it."

"*Love*?"

"Well...I guess lust is the better word."

"That's what I thought. That's why you still have a boner?"

"Yes."

"So.jerk off while I watch."

"Are you sure?"

"This gun is cocked and loaded."

"So is mine."

"So shoot."

The john gave his stiff cock five quick pumps and

he shot his load all over her gorgeous face and glorious tits. Her erect nipples were dripping with his semen. One drop had hit her in the eye. She wiped it out and licked her fingers, the gun still firmly in her other hand's grasp.

"My turn," she said, pulling the trigger. The john screamed and fell to his knees.

The naked whore went downstairs to the kitchen and made herself a tofu sausage sandwich. The john came downstairs and joined her.

"That was intense," he said, sitting down at the little table.

"Yeah, I guess," she shrugged. "Coffee?"

"Sure."

The whore, still naked and glistening with various bodily fluids, none of which were her own, poured the john a cup of coffee. He had put his pants back on and was fully clothed.

"Have you learned your lesson yet?" she asked him.

"Not yet."

"I didn't think so. Take your time. It's your money."

"Speaking of which, I have to get to work," he said.

"Me too," she said.

"See you tomorrow, same time." The john drank some of the coffee, got up, put his badge back on, adjusted his tie, kissed the whore on the check, and left.

"*Next!*" the whore yelled.

Another john came in from the lobby, where several other johns were sitting, reading dirty magazines, putting themselves in the mood.

"Hi there," he said.

"You again," she said. "Okay, go upstairs."

The second john went up to the bedroom and began

removing his clothes.

The whore took a quick shower, then lay on the bed, spread eagle and seductive.

"What would you like this time?" she asked him.

"This time I want you to actually shoot me," he said. "I'm sick of living with myself."

"Are you sure? That costs extra."

"I can pay."

The second john took a wad of cash out of his wallet and laid it on the table.

"That'll cover it," she said.

The whore reached into her own snatch, removed a snub-nose pistol, and shot the second john's cock off, letting him bleed to death on the floor.

As he lay on the floor writhing in agony, she stood over him, so he looked upright inside her dark, moist pussy, as if it were Eternity itself.

"You made me do this," she said. "Because you were bad. Not just to me. But to *all* women."

"I know," he gasped with his dying breath. "I deserve to suffer...finish me. Please."

She nodded and casually put a bullet in his skull. His blood gushed and merged with all the other blood that had already stained the hardwood floor. She scooped up his brains with a paper towel and flushed them down the toilet in the adjacent bathroom.

Since the pistol was still warm, she lay on the bed and masturbated with it till she climaxed.

Then she went down to the lobby and addressed the rest of the johns.

"I'm calling it a night, boys. Take your guilt complexes home and sleep on them. I'll see you tomorrow. I need some rest."

The naked whore went upstairs and slept soundly, the snub nose gun deep inside her snatch, comforting her.

(Originally published in *Out of the Gutter Online*, 2014.)

BEHIND THE BAR

For Mickey

Mick and Chuck were fucked up. Both had been sitting at the bar for some time now. It was late afternoon and the joint was nearly empty, the daily lull between thirsty zombie attacks. It was almost dinnertime, and the place would be full again. People here drank their dinners. Mick and Chuck were having the early bird special, which would normally be called happy hour, but they weren't normal, and they weren't happy, and they'd be here for way more than an hour.

"Don't call me Chuck, I fucking hate that," said Chuck. "Reminds me of Chuck Norris. Chuck Barris. Woodchucks. Fuck all 'em, fuckin' motherchuckers. I ain't no fuckin' Chuck."

"What about Chuck Berry?" said Mick.

"Fuck Chuck Berry, too. He pisses on chicks for kicks."

"Yeah, so?"

"Well, everyone has their good qualities. I still hate rock and roll."

"Well, then don't call me Mick."

"But you *are* a Mick."

"You mean I'm Irish."

"That's the fancy way of putting it, yeah. But you're still a Mick."

"You're still a prick."

"Well, then call me Prick. Just don't call me Chuck.

Call me Hank."

"But that's not your name."

"My name is whatever the fuck I say my name is. And today it's Hank."

"Rhymes with Yank. Like my dick. Listen, I'll call you whatever the fuck I wanna call you, and today I wanna call you Chuck. Tomorrow I may not call you at all, so be grateful."

"Fuck you, Mick. Suck my sick dick."

"Your dick is sick?"

"It's limp and it itches. Must be from this skanky bitch I banged last night."

"So what else is new?"

"How would you know what my dick is like? Because you're a fuckin' actor and fuckin' actors suck fuckin' cock for a living?"

"Hey man, I eat pussy like it's goin' out of style. I don't suck no cock. Not even yours. I ain't one of your fans. I don't even like to read. Only fags like to read, and only fags suck cock. And I ain't no fag."

"Even if you were a broad and had the biggest tits in the world, I *still* wouldn't let you blow me. That mouth has spouted too much stupid dialogue in too many stupid movies. You *should* rinse your mouth out with my genius cum, but you're not worthy. My royal cock deserves better."

"This movie we're doing is basically just a blow job for your ego, right?"

Chuck shrugged with resignation. "Just make sure you swallow it all, bitch."

"Your writing is just jerking off inside people's skulls, anyway. Either that or takin' a shit on their brains. From what I hear."

"You're a fucking actor and you got the fucking nerve to call *me* a jerk-off? *Fuck you!*" Chuck socked Mick in the eye, and Mick fell back off his stool, climbed back up, finished his shot of rye, and ordered another.

"Yeah, fuck you too," said Mick.

"That's it? You ain't even gonna hit me back?"

"I don't beat up old men."

"You mean you just don't want your ass kicked by an old man."

"Yeah, whatever. I don't even know what I'm doing here. I don't even drink."

"I can tell. Fuckin' pussy. Typical actor."

"I'm doing research."

"Research, my ass."

"I'm not that drunk yet, sorry."

"No, you can only get stoned on yourself."

"Hey man, why do you want me to play you in a movie if you don't even like me?"

"Because I hate *my*self."

"Okay, that makes sense."

"You ever get a pimple on your cock?" Chuck asked suddenly.

"Excuse me?"

"A pimple. On your cock. A big, fat juicy pimple that when you popped it, oozed out pus like your cock sprang a leak and was shooting cum out the wrong hole."

"Can't say I have. Why did you have a zit on your cock?"

"Jerking off with margarine."

"I've never done that, either."

"Well, then you haven't lived."

"I used to fuck this chick that liked to pop my ingrown hairs, but that was on my face."

"That is a common fetish," said Chuck. "*All* women like to squeeze 'n' pop ingrown hairs. Like miniature orgasms. I don't get it."

"Neither do I. But I don't get *any*thing women do."

"Neither do I."

Mick and Chuck clinked shot glasses, downed their beer chasers, and then Mick signaled for another round.

"Tell me something," said Mick. "I understand why you used to be a bum because you had no bread before. But now you got a chunk of change from this movie we're making of your life, and you must make a decent living from your books, am I right? So what's with the pathetic act? Just putting me on, part of your professional schtick? Or do you really enjoy suffering?"

Chuck looked at Mick, then hit him squarely in the jaw, knocking him back off his stool. Then Chuck spit on him as he lay on the ground, and said, "Yeah, I thrive on pain. How do *you* like it?"

Mick stood up, sighed, and then hit Chuck hard, right in the nose. Blood burst through Chuck's fingers as he held it and cursed.

"You got blood in my goddamn beer!" Chuck said nasally.

"It's good for you," Mick said. "You're suffering for your art, asshole. Here, finish it." Then he picked up the glass and tossed the liquid in Chuck's face.

Chuck and Mick traded blows as the bartender idly cleaned glasses that didn't really need to be cleaned anymore, but he was bored. A woman sat at the end of the bar watching them. Her hand was under her skirt, between her legs. She masturbated and climaxed just as Chuck and Mick finished their business and sat back down and ordered a fresh round.

"Hold the blood," Mick said, and Chuck laughed.

The woman at the end of the bar was in her fifties, a former beauty queen whose acting career never took off, so she crash-landed here, where she comfortably mingled with the rest of life's local losers.

Chuck looked at her, but she shamefully avoided eye contact. He nudged Mick's shoulder.

"I bet she was a piece of ass back in the day," Chuck said.

"I still wouldn't kick her out of bed now."

"That's because you're a desperate whore."

"So? She probably is, too. And so are you. We're all desperate whores, one way or another."

"Why don't you go make her day? Maybe she'll recognize you from the goddamn movies."

"I'm not that hard up, Chuck."

"Don't call me Chuck."

"How about upchuck?"

"Only after I puke on your corpse. Hey, I'll bet you ten bucks that broad will take you out back and blow you for ten bucks."

"But then if she says yes, I'll just be spending the ten bucks I win and giving it directly to her. What's in that for me?"

"So she gets the ten bucks, and you get a blow job."

"I bet she needs the ten bucks more than I need the blow job. Maybe I'll just give her the ten bucks and skip the blow job."

"So what's in that for you?"

"I don't know. Being a nice person?"

"Fuck that. Maybe she'll blow you for free since you're a famous fuck, and she'll be sucking your success right out of you. Maybe it will do her some good. Change her life. And you'll be ten bucks richer."

"I really don't need ten bucks or a blow job at the moment, Chuck."

"Because you're a famous fucking actor and get all the money and pussy you want, right?"

"Right."

"Now you know," Chuck said.

"Know what?"

"Why I won't give up this lifestyle."

"I still don't get it."

"Because talking about things is more fun than actually doing them. Once you do them, there's nothing left to look forward to."

Mick and Chuck clinked glasses and ordered another round.

"I used to be an amateur boxer," Mick said.

"The way you hit, you're *still* an amateur."

"Maybe I should give up acting and put the gloves back on. I'm bored with it."

"Hope you can act better than you can hit."

"You mean you've never seen any of my movies?"

"Hell no. You ever read any of my books?"

"Not yet. Probably won't. I'll just read the script when it's done. Have you written it yet?"

"I'm writing it as we speak. It's all in my head."

"Your head? Your head's all fucked up."

"Then it'll be perfect."

"I can't believe you've never seen any of my movies, but you called them stupid."

"Because *all* movies are stupid."

"That's like saying all books are stupid."

"No, it's not, because not all books are stupid. Only some are."

"Not yours."

"No."

"So maybe our movie will be stupid, too?"

"Probably."

"So why do it?"

"I don't know. I've already spent the money, anyway."

"On what?"

"I'm drinking it."

"But the drinks are on me and the investors."

"Only today. I'm saving for tomorrow."

"What if there is no tomorrow?"

"Now you know why I'm drinking so much today."

Mick and Chuck clinked shot glasses and ordered another round.

The woman at the end of the bar came over and leaned on Mick's shoulder. "Don't I know you from somewhere?" she said.

"No," said Mick. "I'm nobody."

"How about your friend?" she asked.

"I'm anybody," Chuck said.

"I'll blow you both for ten bucks. Each."

"Where?" asked Mick.

"Behind the bar."

"But what about the bartender?"

"I'll blow him, too," she said.

"How about I just give you thirty bucks and you go sit back down?" Mick said.

"Okay," she said. "But if you ever have an ingrown

hair, I'll pop it for free!"

Mick took out a wad of cash and handed it to her. She kissed him on the cheek and sat back down at the end of the bar. The bartender brought her another gin martini with four olives. It was dinner time and she wanted her salad.

"You're right," Mick said to Chuck. "Sometimes talking about something is more fun than doing it."

"Always," Chuck said.

"Not always," said the bartender suddenly. "I wanted a blow job."

"Who is she?" Mick asked.

"My wife," said the bartender.

(Originally published in *Long Distance Drunks: A Tribute to Charles Bukowski*, Perpetual Motion Machine Publishing, 2014.)

MEANTIME

Miami, 1985

Night. Heat. Sweat.

"I'm tellin' ya, Rico, it was like the god damn Fourth of July in Hell," Crockett said as they sat in his black Ferrari outside the Art Deco mansion in Bal Harbor, waiting for something to happen. His pink sleeveless shirt was soaked with perspiration beneath his heavy white jacket. He dragged on his cigarette with cool aplomb, as if impervious to the humidity.

"I can't believe you never told me about this," Tubbs said, loosening another button on his black silk shirt, wondering why he wore a purple Armani suit in this sweatshop of a city, even if it did suit his undercover profile. "You sayin' you helped take down Tony fuckin' Montana?"

"I was *there*, dude, and I haven't been in a firefight like that since 'Nam," Crockett replied. "I mean, it even beat that melee up in New York a couple of months ago. We've been in some serious situations before, you and me, since you relocated to the Sunshine State, but this one, *Jesus*, just thinking about it makes me wanna crap my pants."

"That wouldn't look so good in them faggoty white trousers, man."

"Yeah, no shit. So to speak. I'm not into earth tones, anyway."

"So tell me about it. We got nothin' else to do on

this stupid-ass stakeout." Tubbs turned down the radio, which had been playing "Silent Running" by Mike and the Mechanics.

"Hey, I like that," Crockett said, turning it back up.

"I thought you were a Jimmy Buffet man."

"We ain't exactly in Margaritaville at the moment, pal."

"I hear that. Though I wouldn't mind me a Tequila Sunrise right about now."

"Hang tight. It'll be dawn soon enough. No bars open for the Breakfast of Champions, though. You'll have to settle for a shot on my boat. And I only stock the cheap stuff, sorry."

"As long as Elvis doesn't mind. That neurotic alligator is one jealous bitch. Anyway, c'mon man, the song's almost over. What was it like tradin' bullets and insults with motherfuckin' Scarface?"

"Scarface?"

"Isn't that what they called him? That's what our snitches called him up in New York after he did that hit on that sucker that was gonna testify against his associates at the U.N."

"Yeah, you don't wanna know what they call *you* around here."

"I can imagine. Goddamn crackers."

Crockett laughed and let out a yawn, then said, "Anyway, yeah. Tony 'Scarface' Montana. He was firing more 'fucks' than ammo. Or at least as many, anyway. They were almost as lethal, too, the way he spit 'em out."

"Yeah, I heard he had quite the mouth on him. You actually make direct contact with him?"

"I fired one of the kill shots, pal. At least I'm pretty

sure I did. The odds were in my favor. I was kinda far behind the first wave of attack."

"Yeah? How many shooters are we talkin' altogether?"

"Hell, it made The Wild Bunch look like look like a goddamn game of Pac-Man. Shit, Rico, I'm tellin' ya, that crazy dude was standin' up at the top of those stairs takin' more direct hits to his vitals than a George Romero zombie. He was completely coked out of his skull. We shoulda just aimed for the brain but he was jerkin' around like a piñata in a hurricane, so we just tried to shred his torso. I don't think the fucker had a heart or else he woulda keeled over after the first barrage. I'm tellin' ya, he looked like a dancing taco!"

"I've heard of guys whacked out to the point where they could take maybe a couple to the chest, but this sounds like you were up against The Terminator, man."

"*He* obviously thought so. After he got nailed a few dozen times he just dropped what looked like a grenade launcher and let us use him for target practice until some badass with shades and a shotgun stepped up behind him out of nowhere and blew a hole in his back the size of Cuba."

"How many other cops were with you?"

"Not just cops. FBI, DEA, pest control, damn, *everybody* got called in for the bust. It was a joint operation that turned into your classic interagency cluster fuck once we all showed up at once. We lost all sense of coordination since right ahead of us was a mob of Bolivian hitmen, mixed in with some undercover ops. Switek and Zito were hanging back like half a mile away, and our wires got crossed in the maze of miscommunication. Nobody knew who anyone was once we got to the mansion, but there was no time to ask any of the players for ID since Montana was armed up the ass with a frickin' military arsenal, and the party had already started. The Bolivians had led us to Montana's mansion, see, after we found his old partner and his sister dead in their home. They were newlyweds, for Chrissake. Word on the street was Montana had the hots for her himself, and this was an act of jealousy, against his best friend. He was one sick, twisted bastard on top of everything else."

"Yeah, I heard she was some fine piece of ass, too."

"She was till somebody chewed up that bodacious body with an Uzi like it was so much shark bait."

"Bolivians or Montana?"

"Not sure. It didn't matter. Nobody with a Latin accent walked out of that place alive."

"So the Bolivians beat you there, obviously."

"Yeah, which was part of the plan. We were hoping they'd do our dirty work for us, and then we'd mop up after, including them. It almost went down that way, except Montana turned out to be a much harder target than anyone anticipated. I mean, this was *one* fuckin' guy against a goddamn *army*, Rico. Unbelievable. I'd never seen anything like it. Good thing we had plenty of backup."

"It's almost like the Bolivians were working with you. Only they didn't know it. Sweet."

"Common enemy, anyway. We let 'em get there first. They were sent by this badass Sosa, you know, the drug lord down in Bolivia that finally got nailed last year."

"Yeah, yeah, Alejandro Sosa. Alex to his friends,

most of which are dead or behind bars by now. That was one beauty of a bust. Too bad he had to get popped in the raid. His inside intel would've taken down whole networks, maybe even the Cartel."

"Don't believe everything you hear, pal. I got a source inside the DEA who told me after a few or maybe ten beers that the Cartel got nervous about all the noise up here and actually hit Sosa right before our boys arrived on the scene. Those swingin' dicks stole bragging rights for this takedown just to make themselves look good to the suits upstairs. *Rah-rah-rah*, go team, all that nationalistic, pseudo-patriotic crap being sold to the public these days, and they're buying it, too. Meantime, everyone on this side of the fence knows that Dutch Reagan is funding the rebels in Nicaragua with some covert arms deal with some rogue nation. This was just another way to deflect attention but I bet that dirty little secret, if true, is about to float to the surface, too. Nobody can hide the truth forever, Rico."

"Just until it's too late to fix it."

"We're both singin' those vice cop blues again, pal."

Tubbs shook his head and sighed. "So you're telling me the Feds didn't even come close to capturing Sosa, he was already a corpse by the time they hit his place in Bolivia?"

"That's the grapevine version anyway, and the grapevine is usually right. Who fuckin' knows? It's *all* a goddamn cover-up, pal. We're just pawns in a rigged game, Rico."

"I heard *that*, Sonny."

"But *damn*, we *almost* beat the big boys to the

punch that time. Looking back, we should've cut the hit squad out of our plans, just picked up Montana on any number of charges we had been building against him, but shit, he had already beaten this tax evasion rap, so we couldn't take him down Capone-style. I guess it went down the only way it could have. That dude would've never taken a deal. He was too fuckin' insane."

"But Montana wound up leading you to Sosa anyway, right?"

"Well, once we all agreed this thing wasn't gonna end politely, we were hoping Montana could hook us up with Sosa indirectly, from any skeletons we could find in his closet. And in fact, that's exactly how it played out. We found just what we needed, all the missing puzzle pieces in one place. Or rather DEA did. Vice got totally cut out of the operation after that, man, as usual. The Feds confiscated all of Montana's secret files once the smoke cleared, which eventually led to the bogus raid in Bolivia, for which they took all the credit, naturally."

"Okay, but back up a bit. You were trailing the Bolivians for how long before they inadvertently led the charge on Montana's digs?"

"We were onto them once they landed at the Miami airport. Izzy told us about this death squad sent up from South America to take out our boy, but initially anyway we wanted to get there first and maybe get him to roll over on Sosa if he survived our own raid, which was a big fuckin' 'if'."

"Sosa's people were also behind that United Nations hit."

"Exactly. Our local kingpin, Frank Lopez, was

already dead by then, along with a dirty cop. Our snitches told us this was Montana's big move up the ladder, and he took over the Miami market from there. One of the Feds' prized informants, Omar Suarez, was the first dude to alert us to this mad dog's existence, after the infamous chainsaw incident over on Ocean Drive."

"Yeah, I heard about that. That was some serious Miami Chainsaw Massacre shit."

"Yeah, it was. I arrived on that scene just in time to see the floor show. Blood and body parts everywhere. Apparently, things went south on a meet with some low-level Colombians. Probably a set-up. Anyway, we knew then that this little Cuban fucker was gonna be a major player to watch. He was actually part of the Mariel boatlift back in '80, we found out later. But he moved up the doper social register so fast we didn't have a chance to nail him before his personal body count hit a hundred, plus like I said he was dealing with a dirty cop, name of Mel Bernstein, who kept covering his tracks. But then Montana took him out along with Lopez, which ironically opened up some leads for us."

"Izzy helped you get a line on Montana? Surprised he never bragged about it."

"He's still scared shitless, man, especially once the Columbians and Bolivians got in the way. I've *never* seen Izzy so freaked out."

"So the Bolivians were absorbed into the overall strategy. Got it. Then what happened to them?"

"The main objective was to take down Montana. Once he fell dead into his indoor pool and literally turned it into a bloodbath, we all suddenly turned on each other. That was *really* the freaky part since like I said, I couldn't tell Fed from foe in that haze of gunfire. It was a total *slaughterhouse*, Rico. Be glad you missed it."

"Hell, *no* I ain't. I got a raging boner just hearin' about it."

"Yeah? Well, save it for Elvis. He'll be hungry for a little sausage snack by the time we get back to the boat."

"Ha ha, motherfucker. You couldn't even measure my manhood with a ruler, you'd need a *yardstick*. But I catch your basic drift. We should just call it a night before it turns into a day again, Sonny. This is gonna be a bust all right, but not in the way we prefer it."

"The way I like it is the sweet rack on this airline stewardess I was supposed to meet for lunch," Crocket said with a grin. "This asshole from Chicago is interfering with my personal time."

"Yeah, Miami or bust. I dig it. But I thought Gina had your kinda bust?"

"Well, she does, but you know it is with workplace romances, pal. They never work out."

"So you broke it off?"

"Yeah, before she could."

"You mean the relationship or your cock?" Tubbs let out a laugh.

Crockett shot him a sharply bemused look, then said, "Yeah, well, I've been wondering why you haven't put the moves on Big Booty Trudy?"

"Why's that, Crockett? All you rednecks sexually segregated down here? I like to mix up the races too, man, any way I can. Besides, like you said. Not cool to fuck where you eat."

"You sayin' you don't dig chowin' down on some

pussy now and again?"

"Don't even mention seafood to me right now. My stomach is growlin' as it is. I'm tellin' you, man. This bullshit is a waste of our motherfuckin' resources."

"Not if Izzy's tip is any good, and they usually are since he knows better than to fuck us up. Apparently, this Frank dude has been operating down here ever since he left the Windy City with a bunch of bodies and blown-up buildings in his wake. He only reached our radar a couple of months ago, but apparently, he's been a Miami operator for some time now, after a brief stopover in Palm Beach."

"He's just a thief, right?"

"Not just a thief, but yeah, that's his main gig. Lately, he's been bolder, whacking out any dumb rich crook that happened to walk in on him holding an armful of their ill-gotten gains, mostly jewels that he fences. I really don't mind him takin' out our garbage for us. Saves us the trouble, but still, it's against the law and shit. This so-called thief has become a regular vigilante now. I almost wish we could just let him do his thing. It would make our lives a whole lot easier."

"Yeah, the word 'easy' ain't in our job description, Crockett. So tell me again why Vice is on this when it sounds more like a Homicide or Robbery case."

"Because for one thing, that pretty blue and green midcentury modern palace down the block belongs to a creep with deep connections we've been trying to nail for the past year or so. In fact, he was a known associate of the late Tony Montana."

"You're kiddin'."

"See, Rico? I was waitin' for just the right moment to relate this particular anecdote. Now seems like the perfect time. This dude we're on, Enrique Salazar, is our missing link to the Cartel, or one of 'em, anyhow. He pretty much picked up right where Montana left off. In fact, we have another common enemy here, meaning Frank and us. That's one reason we're hangin' so far back and peepin' the score through binoculars instead of up close and personal."

"So this cat from Chicago is another of your unwilling allies in the valiant fight against crime, Crockett?"

"Hell, Tubbs, I don't know about 'unwilling.' Word is he's been making quite a tidy little profit ripping off our friendly neighborhood drug dealers for the past few years."

"That's what I call a retirement plan."

"Well, I'm afraid his AARP membership is about to be revoked."

More time passed. Silence. Insects buzzing and biting. Ennui. Wang Chung on the radio.

"Hey, speakin' of outrageous stories, you hear about that crazy shit that went down in L.A. last week?" Tubbs asked Crockett after a few quiet moments.

"You mean when the undercover FBI agent got popped?"

"Yeah, and the freeway chase after. Those chumps drove *the wrong way* up a ramp to escape. And they *did* escape, after causing quite a traffic jam, even by L.A. standards."

"Yeah, for now. I heard they got a line on those bat-shit bastards inside the Secret Service."

"What the *hell*? You're kiddin'."

"No shit, pal, from what I hear…"

"You shouldn't sit on a stakeout with your radio on, dumbfuck," a strong, low voice from behind Crockett suddenly said. Feeling the hard steel of a .45 muzzle on the back of his skull, Crockett immediately stopped talking and lifted his hands.

"Lose it," the stranger commanded Tubbs, who reluctantly tossed the sawed-off shotgun from his lap out of the open car into some nearby tall weeds.

"Don't tell me. Your name is Frank," Crockett said without budging or blinking.

"So you are not entirely stupid, good for you," Frank said. He was tall, muscular, and tan, with a perpetually stern facial expression. He was dressed casually in jeans and a Hawaiian shirt. He pressed the gun to Crockett's temple and cocked the piece. "But do not try to get smart with me. I doubt your dry cleaner can get brain stains out of a pink T-shirt."

"Best back down while you got the chance, chump," Tubbs said, eyeing Frank with practiced intimidation. "You don't know who or what you're messin' with here."

"Actually, yes, I do," Frank said. "You clowns have been tailing me for weeks. What, you think I'm an amateur who could not spot a couple of cops dressed like dandies? You're like two walking neon signs, for Chrissake. What I cannot figure out is whether you are on to me or just the score."

"Both," Crockett said calmly.

"Well, I can help you with one, and it is not going to be me that you can put in the bank."

"Help *us*?" Tubbs said.

"Yes," Frank said in a hiss. "Though I am now having my doubts since it was so goddamn easy to get the drop on you fuckin' idiots. It makes me wonder if you can handle the situation."

"What situation is that, Frank?" Crockett said, keeping his cool, but simmering beneath the surface. "Besides *this* one, I mean."

"Well, while you girls were sitting here gossiping like two queens in a coffee klatch, inside there's an epic orgy in progress with enough mountains of coke and paid pussy lyin' around to make your year's quota in one fell fuckin' swoop."

"That sounds like a set-up," Tubbs said. "Our source told us the house would be empty. Until you showed up to clean out the closets, that is."

"So it's a surprise party," Frank said. "Deal with it."

"We should call for backup," Crockett said.

"I *am* your backup, slick," Frank said. "Now both of you, get your pansy pastel asses out of the car, hands in plain sight."

Crockett and Tubbs obliged, standing pat with their arms raised as Frank carefully trained his cocked .45 on both of them.

"I will let you go get your weapon on one condition," Frank said to Tubbs. "You both go inside first after I give you the layout, make your bust while I cover you, I get what I came for, and then I am out of here."

"We can't let you continue your self-discounted shopping spree in Miami, pal," Crockett said. "It's our sworn civic duty and all that jazz, ya understand, not to let criminals roam around plying their trade on our dime. Taxpayers tend to frown on that sort of thing."

"Then they need to take their grievances out on all the goddamn crooked politicians running the goddamn show into the goddamn ground from behind their cushy goddamn campaign offices," Frank said. "Me? I'm just another non-taxpayer trying to make a dishonest living like everyone else down here. But like I said, I am done after this, at least in this godforsaken city. I clean out this asshole's safe, then I am out West where the sun does not shine by the time that fucking fireball sets on this muggy shithole again tomorrow, or tonight, I should say."

"So you'll agree to leave town," Tubbs said, unimpressed. "That's it?"

"That is a bonus on top of all the powder and whores inside, but yeah, that's it, slick. Take it or leave it."

"We like package deals," Crockett said, "but *you're* the big prize, pal. Chicago PD has been bugging Miami Dade to mail you back, in a box if necessary, for way too long to just let you skate once we finally found you. I admit, it was downright magnanimous of you to take out so many of your fellow public enemies up there at once, same as you've been doing down here, even if it wasn't for purely altruistic reasons, more like a private vendetta that just happened to benefit society at large. I'm sure you'll get a good citizenship medal from the mayor of Chicago. Ours too. You can keep it nice 'n' polished in prison."

"I did my time, slick. Not going back. *Ever*."

"Maybe we can get you a deal, but we'll have to go through proper channels, Frank," Sonny said. "Sorry."

"Then we most definitely do not have a deal," Frank said. "I will walk away right now, take my stash with me, and you will never see me again. And you will walk away with *nothing*."

"What's to prevent us from tracking you down

again?" Tubbs said.

"Because I will be way outside your jurisdiction, Prince."

"*Prince*?" Crockett echoed with a grin as Tubbs grimaced. "Dude, I am actually starting to like you. Okay, since you're holding all the cards at the moment, tell you what. Let me confer with my partner here, and…"

"No time, cowboy," Frank said. "The party inside is almost over. I also heard it would be at his South Beach fuck club, leaving his house unguarded, but they switched gears and decided to stay in and order pizza at the last minute, which complicated my agenda. Otherwise, I would have been in and out already, and you would still be sitting here sharing your paranoid little sour grapes conspiracy theories."

"Not polite to eavesdrop, Frank," Crockett said with a wince.

"You kept me entertained so I figured I would cut you in on this action since you look so sad and bored, and I felt kinda bad about letting you go home empty-handed. Not really, but you accidentally fit into my Plan B. Together we can take them all down. Works out for everybody. But split us up, his designated drivers will definitely get the upper hand."

"Designated drivers?" Tubbs said. "You mean his sober torpedoes standing guard while they fuck around."

"That is correct. I already cased it. They got way too many *pistoleros* on standby to take on without at least three of us. No more time to bullshit. You in or out?"

Crockett looked over at Tubbs, who looked back, paused, then nodded.

"Let's do it," Crockett said.

Tubbs retrieved his shotgun and the three stealthily approached the mansion, sticking to the street shadows.

Once they arrived, Frank led them to a secluded basement window behind some palm trees, which swayed gently in the soft night breeze, and motioned for them to peer inside. The basement was crowded, smoky, and dimly lit, but the general scenario was evident.

Copious copulation. A sensuous sea of nude, premium female flesh. Mounds of uncut cocaine. Cash. Booze. Guns. Lots of everything, something for everyone.

"I count six shooters," Crockett said.

"Figure at least two more on post upstairs," Tubbs said.

"Three," Frank said. "Already checked. Okay…you two should go in the back way, just around that corner, kick it in, and go straight down the stairs. I'll take care of the goons up front, then meet you down there."

"Wait a minute…" Tubbs said, but Frank was already gone.

"Shit," Crockett said.

"We got enough firepower for this?"

"I'd say between us we got about two bullets for each body, so we gotta make 'em count." Crockett checked the chamber of his Bren Ten 10mm. Full clip.

"From what we can see, Salazar and his boys aren't in fighting shape," Tubbs observed. "Dig those chicks, man. I feel exhausted just looking at 'em."

"We'll let them go," Crockett said. "They'll take off once the fireworks start. No room for petty prostitution perps in the paddy wagon."

"They're too hot to pop any way but one way," Tubbs said.

"Keep your dirty little mind on your job, Rico. This ain't gonna be a cakewalk."

As instructed, they crept around the back, where they found one dead bodyguard already, a casualty of Frank's earlier property surveillance, and got ready to rock.

"Cue the music," Tubbs said before they kicked open the door and went inside, guns drawn.

Inside it was very dark, but the sounds of hedonistic revelry beckoned them to their destination downstairs. The 12-inch extended dance mix of "Fade to Grey" by Visage was being played very loudly from a high-end stereo sound system below.

There was no door to open once they arrived at the foot of the staircase. The air was thick with the heady aroma of unbridled sex. A fog machine from inside the basement room was blowing fake fumes, combined with actual marijuana smoke, that billowed into the outer hallway, making the human images within somewhat hazy, though they were illuminated by the swirling lavender-colored lights of a whirling disco ball hanging from the middle of the low ceiling. There was a big screen television in one corner showing XXX porn with the sound off, which paled in comparison to the real-life debauchery on display. The bulky shadows standing pat on the sidelines of those wallowing in wanton indulgence were obviously the professional bystanders, packing heat. The eerie atmosphere and ominous sense of danger were exhilarating, like an ambient narcotic. Or maybe it was just the secondhand pot smoke. Didn't matter.

Showtime.

"Miami Vice, freeze!" Crockett yelled as they burst inside and the stoned guards, who only froze momentarily due to shock, immediately responded with massive volleys of gunfire and expletives, which were almost but not quite drowned out by the pulsating synthesizer beat of "Fade to Grey." There were several other naked, unarmed men wallowing in sleaze, but they only cowered in fear, not posing a threat, and probably not worth any extra bother, random customers caught in the wrong place at the wrong time.

Dozens of shots and screams ensued, beautiful bodies nearly caught in the crossfire. Blood burst from heads and chests onto hysterical high-class hookers, all nude except for shiny, dominatrix-style pumps, their bountiful, bouncing breasts suddenly red and sticky with gore, but not their own. Crockett and Tubbs let the women as well as their johns run past them and back up the stairs as the two intensely focused cops continued moving quickly forward through the room, taking out targets literally left and right. A couple of the high-heeled hookers slipped and fell on the cocaine spread across the floor like flea powder, whipping up minor dust clouds, though most of it was now mixed with various bodily fluids and guts, giving it the consistency of thin, well-whipped pancake batter.

Then Crockett and Tubbs finally found their main objective, Enrique Salazar, his nose covered with what looked like flour, but wasn't, standing in front of a well-stocked, garishly decorated tiki bar, totally naked except for a gold medallion, his penis still erect and glistening from frequent recent use.

"Fuck you, *maricons*!" Salazar shouted, picking up and waving around a .38 sitting next to a bottle of whiskey and a pile of cash on the bar behind him.

"Now where have I heard that before?" Crockett said out loud.

"Déjà vu all over again?" Tubbs said as Salazar aimed the gun at them, about to squeeze the trigger.

"Including this part," Crockett said as he fired a single round through Salazar's forehead. It was his last bullet. Tubbs had already spent his last shell.

With everyone dead or gone, Crockett and Tubbs looked around for Frank, but he was nowhere to be seen.

Stepping over the cocaine-covered corpses, they went back upstairs to the opulent parlor and checked out the equally luxurious living room. No one was around.

Then they went inside what appeared to be an adjacent, wood-paneled office decked out with retro furniture. A safe behind the desk was wide open and as empty as the rest of the house.

Out front, they found exactly what they thought they'd find. Three dead bodies. But no sign of Frank.

"We've been played for a diversionary tactic all along," Tubbs said.

"You heard what he said earlier, right?" Crockett said, holstering his empty gun. "About heading out West where the sun don't shine?"

"I assumed that meant up your cracker ass, but wrong direction, I guess."

"Where out West doesn't the sun shine, Rico?"

Tubbs nodded. "Want me to drop a dime to Seattle PD?"

Crockett shrugged and sighed. "Nah. Fuck it. Dude helped us nail these scumbags. Let's give him a head start, at least."

"And just call it a night, finally. Righteous enough, all things considered. So what do we tell Castillo?"

Crockett shrugged. "Nothin'. We got here, thought we saw a shadow creeping inside, then somebody watching the house made us and forced us into a confrontation. Frank never showed."

"It's like he was never here," Tubbs said.

"That's how it is with most of us, Rico. We're just killing time until it kills us. Nothing we do matters in the long run. We're just going through the motions until…" Crockett stared into the dark but glowing horizon.

"Until what?"

"Until it's finally over."

Sirens wail in the distance. Dawn breaks. The stars slowly fade away. Freeze frame.

(Originally published in *Fast Women and Neon Lights: 1980's inspired mystery, crime, and noir short stories*, Short Stack Books, 2016.)

A HOT NIGHT AT HINKY DINKS

Oakland, CA., 1944

A warm offshore breeze wafted in from San Pablo Avenue through the open double doors, putting all the bar patrons in a tropical mood, despite the arid atmosphere, but also giving some of the more restless drinkers the jitters. It was known as earthquake weather. Anything could happen, at any moment. A blood-red sunset drenched the Bay in ominous hues. "Caravan" by Duke Ellington played obliviously on the jukebox as if everything would be all right.

Hinky Dinks' proprietor and chief bartender Vic Bergeron turned around, reached up, and took down a bottle of J. Wray Nephew rum from the bamboo shelf behind him.

"This is seventeen years old, from Jamaica," he said to his two friends, Ham and Carrie Guild, visiting all the way from Tahiti. They both nodded approvingly as Vic poured two ounces of the premium aged rum into a silver shaker filled with crushed ice, followed by two ounces of Red Heart Jamaican Rum, for the sake of subtle, sublime complexity. He then added the tart juice from two freshly squeezed limes, an ounce of orange Curacao from Holland, a half ounce of Rock Candy Syrup, an ounce of French Orgeat, shook it up well, then poured the combined ingredients into two chilled glasses, also already filled with crushed ice, waiting on the bar. "Just a little something new I've been experimenting with," Vic said with pride.

Ham and Carrie sipped their cocktails tentatively at first, but once the rich, tangy concoction made their taste buds tingle and their brain cells swoon, they enthusiastically expressed how impressed they were with Vic's invention.

"Wait!" Vic said suddenly. "I forgot something. Don't take another sip yet." He reached below the bar, pulled out some springs of fresh mint, and garnished both drinks. It was the perfect final touch on his masterpiece.

"This is delicious," Ham said. "It tastes like the islands!"

Carrie concurred. "Maita'I Roa Ae," she said.

"What?" said Vic with a bemused grin.

"It means 'good' in Tahitian," Carrie explained. "Out of this world!"

"Then that's what I'll call it!" Vic said. "I just hope nobody else tries to steal credit for this formula. I have a feeling it will be my liquid legacy. Keep it to yourselves for now."

Vic then made himself a newly christened Mai Tai with the same formula cut in half, since he couldn't afford to get loaded on the job, and this was strong stuff, as the tiki gods intended. The three chitchatted as they enjoyed Vic's triumphant creation.

Artie Shaw's version of "Temptation" was playing when an exotically beautiful, voluptuously composed young woman of dubious ethnic origin, dressed in a very tight, low-cut flower pattern gown and black high-heeled pumps, strode in and sat down beside Ham and Carrie.

Vic was immediately entranced, as was Ham.

Carrie bristled. The raven-haired stranger's intensely sexual feminine allure was both intoxicating and intimidating. No one noticed that the temperature of the bar had suddenly dropped as a rogue fog bank defied the high-pressure system dominating the region, infusing Hinky Dinks with a light, cool mist, concurrent with the siren's arrival.

"What'll it be, miss?" Vic said, hypnotized by her sensuality while shivering slightly.

"I'll have what they're having," she said in a seductively husky voice.

"It's not for sale," Carrie said curtly. "This is a private party, lady."

"Coming right up," Vic said as he began preparing another Mai Tai.

Carrie glared at the strange woman and noticed her pupils were a deep scarlet.

When her drink was set before her, the woman didn't even take a sip. Instead, she asked, "What's in it?"

As if in a trance, Vic told her the exact ingredients and their precise measurements. Carrie was aghast. Ham just finished his Mai Tai and requested another. Vic complied.

"Aren't you at least going to drink it?" Carrie asked the stranger.

"I never drink…rum," she said.

"Then why did you ask for a cocktail?" Carrie said.

"Because I'm thirsty, but not for alcohol."

The woman then got up from her seat, walked behind the bar, slipped her gown down and off her shapely gams, exposing her large, firm, pointy breasts and impeccably coiffed genitalia, kicked it away, and stood next to Vic wearing nothing but her high heels. Vic was stunned but didn't move as she embraced him, kissed him, and then opened her luscious crimson lips wide to sink her fangs into his throat.

"*Vic!*" Carrie shouted, snapping him out of his daze. Instinctively Vic grabbed a tiki statue off the bar, broke off the corner of its wooden head on the edge of the counter, and impaled the woman in her well-endowed chest with the jagged edge. Blood spurted down her soft, ivory-fleshed torso and rounded hips and all over his authentic Hawaiian aloha shirt.

The entire bar broke into spontaneous applause. But then a burst of staccato machine gunfire immediately spoiled their impromptu celebration as five large men wearing dark pinstripe suits with brightly colored ties barged in, shooting up the jukebox as well as several valuable bottles of rum and a few tiki mugs lining the shelves behind Vic. Everyone ducked for cover, then froze in fear.

A dapper man dressed in an expertly pressed white suit with an open blue shirt and a straw cabana hat walked in casually behind the armed intruders. Vic recognized him as Ernest Raymond Beaumont Gantt, better known these days as Donn Beach, owner of the most successful Polynesian restaurant in Hollywood, Don the Beachcomber.

"I see you met Lorelei," Donn said dryly to Vic, peering over the bar at the curvaceous corpse, bleeding profusely from the wound inflicted by the tiki statue.

"You know her?" Vic said.

"I met her while on vacation in Bermuda, and brought her back home with me," Donn explained. "Even though she hates the sun and never goes outside in the daytime. She shared some native recipes with me. Including a little something I call…the Mai Tai."

"I don't believe it," Vic said. "Next thing you know, Harry Owen will be mixing pineapple juice with cheap rum and grenadine, garnished with a cherry, and calling it a Mai Tai!"

"It's *my* drink, Vic," Donn said. "Well, it was actually Lorelei's, but she's no longer with us, obviously. I first served it ten years ago at my joint down south. It's somewhat different than yours, but it's better. And it was *first*. So just forget you ever mixed that drink, Vic, and my boys here won't have to cruise back some evening and plug you after you've closed up shop – for *good*."

"You'll never get away with this!" Vic said. "Oakland is now the home of the Mai Tai – not just the drive-by!"

"Too late, Vic. Sorry."

"How did you even know about it?" Vic asked, exasperated. "I just started playing around with it last week!"

"Lorelei is my most trusted spy," he said. "Or was, anyway. Now you're a murderer, Vic. No more Mai Tai's for you behind bars."

But then Lorelei's pin-up figure suddenly melted into an oozing pile of gore and mysterious smoke, rendering her body both unrecognizable and unidentifiable. The cool mist engulfing the bar evaporated, and everyone was perspiring once again, but not just from the heat.

"Damn, I didn't see that coming," Donn observed with a grimace. "I guess you're off the hook, Vic. How did you even know she was a…"

"I get around too, you know," Vic said. "I know her kind. *And* yours."

"Listen, why don't we just all have a round of Mai Tai's and talk about this," Donn said. "Maybe we can share the recipe?"

"It died with her," Vic said. "You're not getting it from me."

"Well, can I at least try it?"

Vic looked back at the shelf and the rows of broken bottles, rum dripping down and mixing with the gruesome bodily fluids that had once been Lorelei.

"I guess I got enough left," Vic said. "Have a seat."

Donn and his mob of gun-toting goons occupied the bamboo chairs beside the shell-shocked couple of Ham and Carrie, who had already mutually vowed to never visit the States again.

Soon everyone was drunk and friendly. Donn promised to back off his threat, deciding there was room in the world for more than one Mai Tai recipe.

"Even though mine is the best, if not the original," Vic insisted.

"History will be the judge of that," Donn said with an apathetic shrug, downing his fourth Mai Tai. Donn had bought unlimited rounds of Mai Tais for everyone in the bar, except for one. In a very dark corner of the bar, a werewolf was drinking a Pina Colada. His hair was perfect.

"Sorry I messed up your place," Donn said to Vic in a happy slur. "Violence is not normally my way of doing business."

Vic smiled and said, "Forget it, Donn. It's Oaktown."

Trader Vic's Original Mai Tai Recipe
1 oz amber Martinique rum
1 oz dark Jamaican rum
1 oz fresh lime juice
1/2 oz orgeat syrup
1/2 oz of Cointreau
garnish with mint

(Originally published in *Mixed Up: Cocktail Recipes and Flash Fiction for the Discerning Drinker and Reader*, Skyhorse Publishing, 2017.)

BEAT THIS

A Vic Valentine Vignette

For my friend William Wallace, cheers.

San Francisco, 1997

Sometimes the news is only good when it's compared to the bad news. It's all relative. Unfortunately, the shit sets the standard, or so it seems.

As you can probably discern from that cynical statement—even if you're not an ace detective like me, Vic Valentine, Private Eye—I was at a low point in my life during this period. Of course, the relatively high points weren't exactly going to give me vertigo, either. In fact, I had just broken up with a babe that reminded me of Kim Novak. Okay, she broke up with me, because why would I break up with a babe that looked like Kim Novak, especially since I look nothing like Jimmy Stewart? I'll take whatever I can get. But the fact remained, that I was depressed as hell the day I went to meet a reporter from the *Chronicle* at the Tonga Room in the Fairmont Hotel. I wanted to die. Not by my own hand. Maybe someone would shoot me on the way. Of course, then I'd stand up my date. I didn't think he'd care much, even if I did have a hot tip on a story he had been trying to break open for months.

Since I felt I had nothing to look forward to anymore, even though I was still only in my thirties, I just wanted to hurry up and get everything over with, even stuff I enjoyed, like tiki drinks at a tiki bar. That way I could go on to the next thing, and get that over with, too. Pretty soon I'd have exhausted all possible options, checking off my bucket list, and then I could kick it. The bucket, that is.

William E. Wallace changed my outlook on life, and then some. He might change yours too, if you're still reading this. Hang in there. It gets better. Life, I mean. If you're lucky. A lot of it depends on your attitude. Or so Bill the Thrill taught me.

"Mind if I call you Bill?" I asked him when I sat down at a table near the "pond" in the middle of the massive room, on which floated a raft that sometimes featured a band. Every fifteen or so minutes, a Disneyland-ride-esque "thunderstorm" would strike, augmenting the faux-tropical ambiance. The drinks and food were only so-so, but the presentation was magnificent, kitsch-wise.

"Sure," he said. Even though he was only a little older than me, his handsome face was creased with hard experience. But he still exuded a boyish enthusiasm, at least for his work, which is why we were there. "What's your name again?" he asked.

I told him. He gave me a quizzical look.

"Vic Valentine? Is that your porn name?"

"Um, yeah. I was born with it."

"No. *Porn* name."

"Oh. I thought you said 'born,' as in 'Born Free.'"

"No. I said 'porn,' as in 'free porn.'"

"Okay, well no. I don't do porn."

"I was kidding, anyway."

"Oh. Next time, give me a heads up since you're not that funny."

He already hated me, I could tell. Or so I assumed.

It's a defense mechanism of mine, sort of a preemptive strike. Also, I just happen to rub most people the wrong way.

To my surprise, instead of telling me to fuck off, he simply smiled and nodded and said, "Duly noted." Wow. He was way too congenial to be a hardboiled reporter. But then I had something he wanted, so he put up with me. I was like a sexy gal with an annoying laugh. "So what can you tell me about the dead girl?" he asked me, getting right down to business.

I might as well confess right now: the girl who looked like Kim Novak who broke up with me? She was found dead on the beach up the coast in Marin County. No, I didn't kill her. But since the cops would trace her final days and connect her to me, I might as well come clean now and get my name in the paper as an accomplice. I mean to the good guys.

"She was great in the sack," I said.

He nodded. "Okay. But that doesn't help me solve her murder."

"Are you sure it was a homicide?"

"And rape. Got it straight from the cops."

"Why don't you just let them handle this?"

"I'm on the crime beat. If I can get a scoop on the death of a major wealthy socialite, my byline gets recognition, and I might get a raise."

"She was a wealthy socialite?" Damn, no wonder she dumped me. She was dating far below her station. Of course, there were probably other reasons. But right now this was my favorite. Relieved me of any responsibility and made her seem shallow.

Bill was confused. I often have that effect on people. "You didn't know? I thought you were sleeping with her?"

"Well, she actually spent most of our time together asleep, so we didn't chat much. She seemed pretty depressed most of the time. I got the idea I was merely a distraction from whatever was bugging her. Good enough for me."

"So it was just a sex thing."

"Well, yeah. At least for me. But then sex means a lot to me. I really have nothing better to do when I'm not working. And I don't work that much."

"And for her?"

"Other than free physical therapy? You got me."

"Was it serious between you?"

"No. I mean, not for her."

"For you?"

"I might've been if she hadn't broken it off."

"Broken off what? Your dick?"

He made me laugh. "No, that's still intact. Our so-called relationship, I mean."

"Sounds like you didn't know much about her."

"I guess not. I knew enough once she took her clothes off. All I needed to, anyway. I fall in love easily."

"You mean lust."

"It all distills down to the same base elements."

"Bottom line: you were intimately acquainted, at least physically."

"And emotionally. At least I was. She was always a bit distant. But close enough to touch, so I settled for that."

"I see. I think. So what can you possibly offer me the cops don't already know?"

"This." I pulled a little black book out of my pocket

and handed it to him.

He opened it up and looked inside. "This is a Bible."

"Yeah, I know."

"So she was religious?"

"I have no idea. I mean, at least not enough to not believe in premarital sex, obviously. Though I would've married her in a heartbeat. But she never asked. Anyway, I took this out of her purse when she wasn't looking, because I thought it was an address or phone book, and I was paranoid she was cheating on me. I planned to follow whomever she was dating besides me, to confirm my insecurity. But instead, I found this, which only made sense to me when I heard about her death through the grapevine. Look at the passage she highlighted." I took the tiny Bible from him, and opened it to this famous quote: "*He that is without sin among you, let him cast the first stone at her.*"

He thought about it a moment, then asked, "Are you religious?"

"I worship the Holy Trinity of Frank, Dean, and Sammy," I said.

"I'll take that as a 'no.'"

"I did go to Catholic School back in Brooklyn. I remember that particular quote because it was from one of my favorite parts of the Bible."

"Why?"

"It's about sex."

"Adultery, to be exact."

"Okay. I thought she was a hooker?"

"You don't pay much attention when you read, do you?"

"Even when I don't. Which is most of the time."

44

"Obviously. You read my piece on this, I assume. That's why you contacted me?"

"Yes."

"I said in the first line she was a wealthy socialite."

"Okay, I only scanned it. I was in the bathroom at the time, and busy."

"Hope you didn't shit on my article."

"No. I was beating off."

"*Whoa.* TMI."

"Sorry. I didn't get any on your article, though. I used toilet paper to wipe my hands."

"Um, let's get back to the original topic here."

"Same topic. I was thinking of her at the time."

"You mean while reading her obituary."

"Kinky, right? Zombie sex."

"That's called necrophilia."

"Well, she was alive in my head. Still is."

"You said you initially heard about her death through, as you call it, 'the grapevine'."

"Right."

"Who is that, exactly?"

"Actually, it's not a network. It's a dude. Doc Schlock, also known as Curtis Jackson. He owns a joint called The Drive-Inn, over in the Richmond."

"Yes, I know the place. Never been inside. It's a bar that also rents videos, right?"

"Yeah."

"I'll have to check it out sometime. So how did this 'Doc' know she was dead?"

"He heard it from a friend."

"What friend?"

"Someone on the inside."

"Inside of what?"

"You know. People that know about that stuff."

"You mean the police?"

"Could be."

"You're setting yourself up as a suspect, you know."

"That's actually the opposite of my intention."

After considering this information some more, he pointed to the tiny Bible and asked, "How is this significant, do you think?"

"No clue. You're the reporter."

"You're the detective."

"Yeah, but you're like, y'know. Professional 'n' shit."

"And you're not?"

"I try to be. I can't think of anything else to do. My vocational options have all dried up."

"Try harder, then. That passage concerns an adulteress. You did know she was married, right?"

"What?" No wonder she never proposed to me! Conflict of interest combined with mild disdain. "You're kidding!"

"Jesus, did you two ever even have a conversation?"

"Not really. I met her at The Drive-Inn one night. She was totally loaded, and I was going to call her a cab. But then she passed out, so I took her upstairs."

"To the attic?"

"No, my apartment. I rent a place above The Drive-Inn. Doc is my landlord."

"And you date raped her?"

I nearly spit out my Mai Tai. "No! I mean…she woke up, started to undress, and then…Nature took its course."

"Nature?"

"Yeah, I mean, she got naked, crawled into my bed, asked me to join her, so I did. I never turn down free sex. Or a free drink. This is on the Chronicle's tab, yes?"

"Depends on the lead. Can I keep this?"

"Go and sin some more," I said. Then I got up and walked out so I wouldn't get stuck with the bill. I knew he'd be in touch.

It didn't take long. Later that night, he called me at home.

"Cops just told me they found two semen samples inside her dead vagina. They're running DNA tests now."

"Stop before you turn me on."

"When was the last time you saw her, and by 'saw,' I mean screwed?"

Uh, oh. "Shit…"

"Yup. They'll be knocking on your door any minute now."

Just then there was a knock on the door to my office. Swear to Sinatra.

I sighed. "They beat you to it, man. Sorry, you didn't get to break the case."

"Is that an admission of guilt?"

"Of killing her? No. Fucking her the night before she was found dead? Yes. She woke up in my bed here, in fact. That's when she told me we had to stop seeing each other. Now I know the real reason. She probably feared for her life." Despite the tragic circumstances, my fragile ego had never felt sturdier.

The pounding on the door was so loud now even he could hear it on the other end of the line. "Sounds like you're screwed in more ways than one, buddy."

"Yeah, I guess. But you did say there was another sample inside of her, so I'm only one of two suspects."

"You better get that. I'll meet you down at the station. I'll bring the Bible with me."

"Yeah, I'm about to get religion myself."

I hung up and was about to open the door when it got kicked in.

Standing there was a tall, middle-aged man, pretty handsome if you're into that kind of thing. In fact, he sort of looked like Jimmy Stewart. Not nearly as nice, though. He was holding some kind of a tool.

Even a shitty detective like me could figure out this was her husband. I also assumed the other semen sample was his. Our sperm had mingled inside of the corpse of his late wife. I tried to suppress my boner. His opening statement helped considerably in that regard.

"I'm going to sign your death warrant with a ballpoint hammer," he said.

"You mean ball *peen* hammer, you idiot."

"No, I didn't. Wait, did I? No, no. That works. Get it?"

"Yeah, I got it, all right."

Then I reached into my desk and pulled out my .38. That didn't stop him. He threw the hammer at me and I ducked, but also dropped my gun in the process. It went off but the bullet didn't hit anything besides the wall. Meantime, the flying hammer crashed through the window behind me. Then the intruder lunged at me over the desk, strangling me.

The cops showed up right behind him. They'd been there to book me, but instead, they nailed the actual culprit.

Naturally, I took all the credit, telling them I'd lured him to my office so they could make the bust. They weren't buying it, but that's how I told it to Doc and any pretty girl that would listen, anyway.

Anyway, after they grilled me down at the local precinct, they let me go, but with an admission not to leave town pending further questioning. They obviously felt confident they had their man already, though. My reporter friend never showed up, though.

The next day, Bill called me. He was downstairs at the bar. Doc was serving him a cocktail chased by a beer. It obviously wasn't his first for the day. Up on the TV behind the bar, Doc was playing *Chinatown.*

When I sat down, Bill tossed that morning's edition of the *Chronicle* in front of me. "I still got the scoop," he said.

I checked out the headline. HUSBAND ARRESTED IN MURDER OF WEALTHY SOCIALITE.

"You get the byline, after all. Congrats." I scanned it for any mention of my participation in this case. None.

"I figured if I put 'wealthy socialite' in the headline you'd actually notice that detail this time," Bill said.

"How come I didn't get any credit?"

"For what?"

"I helped you break the case, right?"

He shook his head and laughed. "Vic, I wrote that story and turned it in right after we met. I figured it was the husband that underlined that passage, not her. He was their main suspect, anyway. The two semen samples complicated their case a bit, but I knew they'd trace it back to you, and to him. He knew it, too. But

49

first, he'd want a piece of you, the man fucking his wife."

My heart stopped. I felt like the worst person on the planet. Well, one of them. "She died because of me?"

He nodded matter-of-factly. "Pretty much. Indirectly, anyway. You weren't her first affair, but you were her last. The guy was obsessed with her. He'd been following her for weeks. I'm surprised he never tried to kill you both sooner. My hunch is, he wanted to kill her first, then kill you, too. Or maybe even frame you."

"Yeah? How?"

Bill reached into his pocket and handed me back the Bible. "Get a load of this other passage he highlighted."

I did. It was Matthew 5:38-42 in the New Testament. Jesus again: "*Ye have heard that it hath been said, An eye for an eye, and a tooth for a tooth.*" There was more to it, but it had been highlighted out of context with a yellow marker.

"But what about the rest of the quote!" I read it out loud: "*But I say unto you, That ye resist not evil: but whosoever shall smite thee on thy right cheek, turn to him the other also.*"

Bill shrugged and said, "I guess he was a lazy reader. Just like you."

Then he finished his drink, stood up, a bit tipsy, slapped me on the shoulder, and said to me, "Whatever is going to eventually kill each of us is out there right now, or maybe already lurking inside us, waiting. So watch your back and live it up, kid." I got a chill that still resonates deep in the pit of my soul.

I never forgot that parting admonition. In fact, I

thought of it often, whenever I felt like giving up on life after it gave me yet another beating. Those ominous words always haunted me. Especially when I read that Bill had died of cancer, years later, after fighting valiantly to beat it.

(Originally published in *Deadlines: A Tribute to William E. Wallace,* Shotgun Honey, 2017.)

THAT'S A WRAP

The beautiful young red-haired naked girl with the broken kneecaps crawled across the floor, leaving a trail of blood and suds (since she had been in the shower) as she pleaded for her life, finally reaching up for the telephone on the side table next to the plush sofa. The very large well-dressed man with the baseball bat responded by breaking her left arm, making her scream in agony and collapse into semi-consciousness. Earth Kitt could be heard singing "Santa Baby" on Pandora as if everything was just peachy.

"Merry Fucking Christmas, bitch," said the equally beautiful but far less traumatized brunette woman standing in the hallway, watching. "Your present is your life, as long as you stay the fuck away from that audition tomorrow, even on crutches. Happy Fucking New Year, you fucking *cunt.*"

The large well-dressed man and the beautiful brunette woman with intact kneecaps walked out of the penthouse apartment, which loomed high above Sunset Boulevard. The red-haired naked girl with the broken kneecaps and busted left arm lived there with three other roommates, all of whom were out of town for the holidays. She had been dating the director of a new film and everyone assumed she would get the lead role, including the director.

A few miles away in the Hollywood Hills, he was also lying semi-conscious on the floor with broken kneecaps, next to a blood-soaked script that was about to be re-written by new investors.

The next morning the beautiful brunette woman with intact kneecaps showed up for her audition and nailed it—after the new director nailed her, of course. The original director had been hastily replaced due to the severity of his sudden, undisclosed "medical condition."

The beautiful woman was thirty-five years old, which for a female was ancient in this town, in this business. That's why her driver's license claimed she was ten years younger, and due to her smoldering sensuous looks enhanced by lots of makeup and some surgery, she could get away with it. But then her driver's license also displayed her stage name, Miranda Mercedes, even though her birth name was Tina Romano.

Her father was Tony "the Tiger" Romano, a lieutenant for a prominent New York organization once commonly referred to as The Mafia. Now it is considered just another branch of local government since most of the members had successfully assimilated into the business community, thanks to politically financed camouflage.

Of course, nobody in the greater Los Angeles area knew this, although anyone unfortunate enough to engage her in fair competition for anything she wanted was rudely introduced to one of her father's West Coast employees. Then they belatedly suspected they had accidentally stepped on the wrong toes, most likely planted somewhere near the Eastern seaboard. The fact that her own private "bodyguards" often accompanied Miranda to auditions had become a whispered warning to casting directors, agents, and producers around town over the past decade.

Of course, Miranda often resorted to her own feminine wiles to land roles she was clearly unsuited for, at least talent-wise, since she couldn't act her way out of a gushing geyser. She had literally bullied her way into a "career," mostly in B movies that went straight to cable or Blu-Ray, lest her upwardly mobile tactics attract more powerful attention in the higher Hollywood hierarchy. Initially, she has been a porn actress, first in New York, working for her father, and later in Los Angeles.

Rather than resorting to violence, she often employed techniques from this trade behind the scenes in order to land more "prestigious roles" in "legitimate" pictures that featured only soft-core sex scenes but were otherwise well-scripted stories, like *Werewolf Bitches In Heat* and *Vampire Whores of Babylon*. Intimidation or intimacy, whichever worked. That was her motto.

Eventually, her proclivity towards promiscuity in pursuit of her professional dreams, along with comfort in fully exposing and exploiting her own voluptuous body before the camera, *any* camera, resulted in her developing a cult following amongst perverts as well as a killer reputation within the industry, literally.

The kneecap incidents became an urban legend, sending the female victim back to her home in a small Canadian town, crippled for life; and the male victim, her former lover, into therapy, both physical and mental.

Now, enough was enough.

After this final atrocity—one of dozens that were never reported to authorities and only shared

surreptitiously via the inside Hollywood grapevine—
Miranda was finally blacklisted from every single
casting call in the city, even from Z-grade productions.
The timing couldn't be worse from her point of view
since she was planning to segue into even more
respectable, higher profile films, spring-boarding off
her ten-year resume, however illicitly, she had
accumulated her questionable credits. She could only
pass for twenty-five for so long, even with the regular
cosmetic touchups. At least her big boobs were still
real and perky, unlike many aging actresses in her
social circles. But even those succulent, slowly
sagging mounds of feminine flesh couldn't help her get
her nipple in the door anymore.

Even her father couldn't help her, not since the
indictment of his whole crew by a crusading new
district attorney in league with some Trump-sucking
stormtroopers in the F.B.I. However, due to her trust
fund, which had been activated even though her father
was still alive, albeit on his way to life in prison, she
wouldn't have to worry about starving. Just incessant
humiliation and the death of her youthful ambition to
make an identity for herself besides "Mob brat."
Which was even worse. She had been a high school
beauty queen back in Queens and was a model in
Manhattan before moving out West to become a movie
star. It hadn't panned out quite the way she wanted.
Now it seemed it was all over. She'd probably wind up
moving back home and marrying one of her father's
henchmen and raising a bunch of obnoxious sociopaths
like herself. It was a vicious cycle she had tried very
hard to break. But the only thing broken was her spirit.

She decided to stick around and see if her luck

would change before totally giving up. She had made it this far, so why not? You never know what's lurking just around that corner.

As it turned out, her destiny did take a sharp, unexpected turn, just as she had hoped, if not exactly the way she wanted.

Nearly a year after the kneecap incident, Miranda's agent—who was also a West Coast Mob lawyer, not coincidentally, though he wasn't directly handling her father's defense—finally called her with an audition, for which she had been personally requested.

It was for a modern remake of the 1954 holiday classic *White Christmas*, starring Bing Crosby. Or so it was assumed, since the audition consisted of two actresses performing a duet from the movie, "Sisters," originally sung by Rosemary Clooney and Vera-Ellen.

"I've never even seen that stupid fucking movie," Miranda said, lying in bed, hung-over, beside a hunk of a male whose name escaped her, but whose bodily essence had stickily dried on her thighs and lips overnight.

"Doesn't matter, the remake will probably be modernized," said her agent, whose name was Sid Stein. He was nearly eighty years old, but his vitality was matchless. His Mob connections were well-known, but never discussed. Within the industry, he was infamous, often referred to as "Horse Head" with a mixture of awe and fear, which is exactly what he wanted.

"I can't even sing," Miranda said drowsily. "Plus I never even *heard* of that stupid song."

"You can't act either," Sid reminded her.

"Just call Bruno," Miranda yawned. The hunk

beside her stirred restlessly, aroused by the conversation, who then continued snoring. She got up with her cell phone and paced in the nude, groggy, and sticky, after lighting a cigarette, which she smoked as she headed into the kitchen to make coffee. It was then she realized she wasn't even in her own house.

"I keep telling you, Bruno is back in Brooklyn," Sid said. "Your father put the kibosh on all that shit, remember? He's about to suffer the trial of his life. I doubt our people can save him this time. The Feds have too much on him. He will probably be indicted unless certain deals can be made, and, well, some other stuff buried."

"Maybe I should just go see him," she said drowsily, opening cabinets, and looking for coffee grounds. She found some cocaine and sniffed that instead. Same effect as caffeine, only more potent.

"No, he's in custody. You won't be allowed anywhere near him. Just wait. We're working as hard as we can behind the scenes. Your best bet is to continue making him proud, and the best way to do that is to take opportunities as they arise, so to speak."

"Who's making it? Can I just blow somebody?"

"Your reputation precedes you everywhere, sweetheart. Even those lethal lips of yours. Nobody trusts you won't just bite it off now. We can't do it that way anymore. But this is straight up. And the director asked for you specifically. He's a big fan of yours."

"You're kidding."

"No, actually, I'm not. I got this from the director myself. He just called me, in fact."

"What's his name?"

"Nobody you'd know. In fact, nobody *I* know. He

didn't even tell me his name. He just gave me the address of the audition at a warehouse down in Santa Monica."

"Okay, what the fuck, Sid? In our business that's commonly known as a 'set-up.'"

"Oh, grow up, will you? Nobody wants to knock you off, sweetheart. Besides, I had this guy vetted already."

"I thought you didn't even know his name?"

"He *thinks* I don't. But he must know that I know everybody in this town, and those I don't know, get known quickly if I so choose. And I so chose. He's clean, and he's good. This is his first project, and it's for a major studio, according to my sources. All I can tell you is he's just going by the name 'Billy' for now."

"What the fuck is he, twelve? What else has he done?"

"Does it matter? You don't even need to learn the song. You'll do it cold, karaoke style. He already thinks you're ideal for his vision of the role, though again, he wouldn't be specific. The project, whatever the hell it is, has the green light, and these days, when you see a green light, you hit the gas and keep going, doesn't matter who gets run down in the intersection. This is a very exclusive offer, sweetheart, and you're a shoo-in. This will make you not only completely legit, but popular again, and with the right people. People that matter. Oscar-winners, festival judges, critics, self-important asshole gatekeepers like that. This is the best thing that could possibly happen to you, trust me. Just be at the address I texted you today at two."

"In the afternoon?"

"If I meant two in the morning, that *would* be a set-up," Sid said with a laugh.

Miranda glanced up at the starburst-shaped clock on the wall and groaned. It was nearly noon. The house resembled a midcentury modern showroom. Whoever she fucked was obviously rich. She had a type, after all. Then she saw his picture on a wall and felt nauseous. He was a hunk of meat all right, but he had a face that looked like a pockmarked baboon. And now his simian semen was all up inside of her, dripping down her shapely legs. She decided to stop drinking and just stick to drugs from now on.

Then she looked outside and realized she was in Palm Springs. She had two hours to get back to L.A. She threw on her flimsy leopard pattern dress and snake-skinned high-heeled pumps, then began liberally applying lipstick and makeup as she ran outside to her Ferrari parked on the curb. Her hair looked like a fright wig but many men found that just-got-out-of-bed look sexy, since it looked like she'd just had several orgasms before passing out cold. And that was almost always the case. She hoped this director would find her messy hair a turn-on, too. It would save them both a lot of trouble.

The warehouse was located on Pico Boulevard. It had once been part of an independent film studio that had long since folded. Now it was rented out by the landlord for private parties and porn shoots. That's why the floor was so sticky, stickier than Miranda's thighs.

Miranda cautiously entered the warehouse – which resembled an airport hangar, only smaller—after parking in the otherwise empty lot next to it. Her footsteps echoed within the cavernous confines of the hollow space. There was literally nothing inside except two chairs, one of which was occupied by a buxom young blonde whom Miranda immediately recognized, but only acknowledged with a glare and a nod. The tension between them was palpable. They had not been expecting to see each other here, or anywhere, at least anytime soon, since they both went out of their way to avoid each other, given their common history.

In front of the two chairs was a MacBook sitting open on a small table. The "Sisters" scene from *White Christmas* was playing on a loop.

Miranda sat down tentatively and was instantly startled by an omniscient voice emanating from somewhere, seemingly everywhere. Actually, it came from a microphone located in a booth above the room. A dark shadow of a male figure was obviously at the controls, but he remained mostly hidden from their view.

"What the fuck is this, a James Bond movie?" Miranda shouted.

"Please, Miss Mercedes. Remained seated. All will be revealed. I simply want you to read the lyrics now scrolling across that screen."

Apparently, the MacBook was remotely rigged to respond to his controls up in the booth. The "Sisters" scene had indeed been replaced with a karaoke-type scroll.

"You take the Rosemary party, Miss Mercedes. Miss Garson, you take the Vera-Ellen part."

"Fuck this, I'm outta here," Miranda said, rising to leave.

"You will become a global star if you are cast in this role," the voice said. "Trust me. I have the connections.

But they must remain anonymous for now, for reasons I cannot divulge. You have been personally selected by the producer to audition for this part. Your call."

Miranda sat back down, and then both began rotely reciting the song lyrics. The blonde actress at least attempted to stay in tune. Miranda didn't even bother. She just wanted to get this over with as quickly as possible.

"Congratulations, you got the part!" Sid told her the next morning.

"Yeah, yeah, no surprise, since it was just me and one other bitch that showed up, and he needs two bitches to sing that stupid song. I never even *met* the fucking guy. He stayed up in this booth the whole time while we just read the lyrics off a computer. I didn't even sing 'em, since, as you well know, *I can't fucking sing*."

"Doesn't matter, sweetheart. That's how auditions work sometimes. The director just needs to confirm his own instincts. Or hers. Basically, you got the organic quality he needs."

"Desperation?"

"Sure! Whatever works. The other girl had already been cast, actually. He just wanted to get a sense of your chemistry with her on film. I've seen the audition tape. It's marvelous!"

"What the fuck is going on here, Sid? And that other fucking bitch *hates* me, and I fucking hate her right back! Her name is Greta. I used to run into her at auditions all the time. She avoided me like the plague. I don't think we can work together, Sid, I honestly don't. That mystery director needs his fucking head examined. Or better yet, bashed in."

"He wants to meet you both up at a possible location in Big Bear this weekend. A cabin. It just snowed up there, so it'll be bee-*yoo*tiful."

"Aw shit, Sid. Way the fuck up in the mountains? *Nobody* shoots out in the fucking sticks, it's cold and it *sucks*!"

"You do if you need lots of snow for your backdrop! I guess he's moving the action from Vermont to California. The song 'White Christmas' was actually written in L.A. during a heat wave, since the guy who wrote it, Irving Berlin, was nostalgic for his childhood winters. Did you know that?"

"Didn't know, still don't give a festive fuck. I don't want to go all the way up there."

"C'mon, it's great. They shot that old B movie 'The Werewolf' up there, years ago."

"You mean the one where the dude goes to London 'n' shit?"

"I said it was shot around Big *Bear*, not Big *Ben.* Never mind. Just be at the address I just texted you tomorrow night by six…"

Driving up the barren highway into the remote mountains, which had only recently been cleared for car travel, Miranda noticed only one other car on the road. The blonde hair of the driver convinced her it was her co-star, Greta Garson.

Greta and her had once been lovers until they got called for the same audition. Rather than have Bruno scare her off, Miranda didn't even show up for the audition. She actually liked Greta, or having sex with her anyway. They even experienced a tinge of nostalgic lust at the audition, but otherwise didn't speak to one another. Miranda was still bitter, and

Greta was still gloating.

Because of that one audition, and the fact Greta was cast in a movie that turned out to be an award-winning indie sensation, she became a sought-after actress, a big success, dating big-name directors and movie stars, her pictures in all the magazines, while Miranda was left toiling in relative obscurity.

Now Greta was going to share a screen with her, only she'd probably get top billing, since she was the box office draw, if only by default. No way did she deserve that.

"No. Fucking. Way."

Miranda sped up as the two cars were approaching a sharp curve on a steep cliff, then she rammed the bumper and the other car went flying over the edge, crashing and burning into the forests far, far below.

"Now you'll be a legend, like James Dean, you dead fucking *whore*!"

A few miles further, her GPS confirmed she'd arrived at her destination. The snow-laden cabin looked like something out of an idyllic postcard. Too good to be true. Like most things in life.

The door was open so she just walked in. Nobody answered her knock, anyway. This was already looking bad.

Inside the cabin, it was very dark except for the dim glow of a single light bulb dangling from the ceiling in the center of the room, as well as a Christmas tree that was decorated with those old-fashioned big light bulbs, the kind that often caused fires back in the day.

A shadowy silhouette stood in the far corner of the room. The flames from the fireplace barely illuminated his presence. Miranda quickly surveyed the situation as panic began gripping her heart. The single room was sparsely furnished except for a bed in the corner, and a poorly stocked kitchenette. There was also a tiny bathroom. Beside the fireplace was a wooden walking cane leaning against the bricks, just like in the final scene of *Miracle on 34th Street*, one of the few holiday movies she'd actually seen since it was her father's favorite. The smoky aroma from the burning logs would've conveyed seasonal coziness if the rest of the place wasn't so desolate and creepy.

"It's me, Billy," whispered the shadow. "Sit in that rocking chair. Please. Let's get started." She noticed a digital camera perched on a tripod next to the rocking chair.

"Um, shouldn't we wait for the other actress?" Miranda asked, her voice quivering. *The one that just died in a tragic car accident…*

"*What* other actress? Didn't Sid tell you? I'm hiring you for *both* parts. I told the other girl I didn't need her after all. She was only there to sing the song with you. It was a formality since I already knew you were the one I wanted. You see, I'm recasting you in both Lynne Griffin's *and* Margot Kidder's roles. They were in my favorite scenes, you see. *Death* scenes."

Miranda took a moment to process the fact she had run a completely innocent stranger off a cliff, simply for resembling her true target. Then she snapped back to the present since what was done was done. Even though she was wealthy, she could never afford a conscience, since it too often came at the expense of her ambitions. "*Who*? Sorry, I thought we were supposed to be George Clooney's aunt and some other stupid fucking bitch I never heard of who did that stupid fucking number in that stupid fucking movie."

"Just sit in the chair. Please." His voice was alarmingly calm.

That's when Miranda noticed a one-sheet poster on the wall, for a movie she'd never even heard of, depicting a woman in a chair with a plastic bag tied tightly around her head.

She screamed and ran for the door, but he blocked her, and hit her once, dazing her enough so she was limp when he dragged her to the chair and tied her to it.

Before she could scream again, her head was ensnared in a large, heavy-duty, clear plastic bag. Despite her hysterical struggle, Billy tightened it around her throat until she passed out, then he carried her to the rickety bed across the room, where he stripped her nude, except for the plastic around her head, then strapped her to the posts. He mumbled the word "Agnes" as he suckled her nipples, and then again as he climaxed on her warm belly, and tenderly massaged the fluids into her supple skin.

When she regained consciousness a few moments later, he was still straddling her with his pants down around his ankles, except now he was holding a huge butcher knife with both hands, poised to penetrate her torso. Additionally, he was wearing a red wig, framing his vaguely familiar face in long, wavy locks.

Mercedes' screams were muffled by the plastic, which also obscured her vision somewhat. But not enough to avoid the impending horror of her own brutal murder.

"You're right, I am remaking a classic holiday movie," Billy said in a calm, steady voice. "But you got the color wrong. You see, I'm not remaking 'White Christmas.' I'm recreating my favorite scenes from my own favorite holiday movie… '*Black* Christmas.' It was made in 1974 by the man who later directed 'A Christmas Story,' Bob Clark. Isn't that ironic? He inspired me to become a filmmaker myself. And I tried, I tried so very hard, but I failed. Now I make movies just for me. It's my favorite movie ever. My sister and I watched it every Christmas, even after our parents died. After we killed them. Then we became lovers. She was the only woman I ever loved, or made love to. None of the men I loved could compete with her, so I killed them too. We moved to California five years ago, to escape the past and have a future together here, but…it didn't work out. Now nothing matters anymore. Nothing except this film. My *masterpiece*. I am going to upload it to the Internet and millions will see it! It is better than the original because it's all *real*. It's a tribute to my sister, and we will watch it together, again and again. But you also inspired it, you see, so you should star in it. It will make you *famous*."

Though the thick plastic obscured his visage, Miranda suddenly recognized him, and how she knew him. But it was too late.

His eyes widened into a cold, evil stare that sliced through her flesh and into her soul, if she had one, chilling her to the bone because they reflected her fate. Then with a discordant cry of rage and relief, he plunged the knife repeatedly into her chest as she gasped for breath then coughed up blood inside the plastic bag still tied around her neck.

Now Billy's secret contract with Sid—whom he had met at various shindigs around town before his psychotic break—had finally been fulfilled. Mercedes was dead. Her father wouldn't have to worry about her series of crimes leading back to him while he was on trial for numerous unrelated charges. It was the last thing he needed. That family tie had been cut for good. And her death would be blamed on a maniac who could offer no sensible defense. That's why he was paid so handsomely. He'd never get a chance to spend any of it. The police were already on their way up to the cabin after receiving an anonymous tip that a demented killer was holed up inside with his latest victim. Sid had thoroughly "vetted" his patsy, all right.

But as far as Billy was concerned, his real work was just beginning. He removed the digital camera from its tripod beside the bed so he could upload the precious, gory, lurid footage to his laptop and begin editing it for final upload, right after he delivered two very important messages. Billy had done his due diligence as well.

The first email included a full confession with an audio file attached, which had surreptitiously recorded his conversations with Sid, incriminating him as an accomplice in these deaths beyond the shadow of any potential doubts. Even if he hadn't been complicit in this particular crime—in fact, its mastermind—he did hire Bruno the Enforcer to viciously assault and dissuade all of Miranda's foes and competitors, including him. So it was only fair. In fact, Billy even credited Sid as the "executive producer" of the *Black Christmas* remake, disregarding the inferior 2006 version, which Billy never bothered to watch.

After sending the audio file, Billy began composing a celebratory email to his sister, "Agnes," up in

Canada, to let her know the film had finally been completed and was about to make its world premiere this very night, on Christmas Eve. She was still wheelchair-bound after what had happened the previous Christmas. He had recovered from his own injuries that he suffered the same day, at the same hands, though he still walked with a limp. His sister couldn't even type due to the damage done to her left hand, because she was left-handed. Or had been.

The very last image Miranda (barely) saw as her life leaked out of her onto the cold mattress was a one-sheet on the wall for Brian De Palma's first hit movie, *Sisters*, from 1973, starring Margot Kidder as a model suffering from split personalities, one of which happens to be homicidal.

(Originally published in *It's A Weird Winter Wonderland*, Coffin Hop Press, 2017.)

FISH OUT OF WATER

Seattle, 1958

The big man wearing a trench coat over his hulking physique and a Fedora on his domed skull avoided all eye contact as he navigated the bustling crowds at Pike Place Market, hoping no one noticed that his ripped pants barely fit his massive legs, or that his shoes had been stretched and torn in his attempt to cover his large, apparently deformed feet.

His face was even worse. That's why he kept his head down. But his intimidating bulk and mysterious presence caused quiet alarm amongst the passersby, most of whom dismissed him as a vagrant.

Sinatra was singing "Witchcraft" from the radio of a brand new Ford Thunderbird parked near the fish market, where the big man was loitering, attracted by the scent of fresh seafood. But he had no money. This festive, colorful environment was completely foreign to his sensibilities and experience.

No longer able to withstand his hunger pangs, the big man intercepted a large tuna being flung through the air between the merchants as part of the entertainment for the tourists gathered around the display. In the process, his hat flew off, fully revealing his face.

Everyone scattered. A woman screamed. A police patrol car parked down the block was alerted by the commotion and began approaching the frantic scene, sirens wailing.

The big man picked up his hat and ran with the tuna beneath his arm as he fled up Pike Street several blocks, knocking people over like they were bowling pins, finally making a right on Third Avenue, leaving frightened pedestrians in his wake. The police weren't far behind. A citywide bulletin had already been issued. The authorities were on the lookout for the hideous homeless giant.

The big man finally stopped in a heavily shadowed, deserted alley in Pioneer Square. It was now dusk so very light illuminated his temporary sanctuary. Breathing heavily, he finally began devouring his stolen catch.

He had only been there a few moments when he heard a single female crying out in terror and assumed someone had spotted him. But when he turned to locate the source of the scream, further down the alley, he only saw a young woman being viciously assaulted by a gang of leather-jacketed thugs with greasy hair, three with their jeans pulled down around their ankles, another already on top of her.

Instinctively, the man lumbered toward the scene and began tossing the four assailants aside as the girl, shivering in the cold, misty air, covered up her violated body with the remnants of her clothes, which had been torn off in the course of the attack.

The teenage rapists began jumping on the man, cussing, and stabbing him with switchblades, but his prowess was overwhelming. Bones cracked and flesh bled as the big man fought off the gang, and within less than a minute they were all limping away in painful retreat.

The big man carried the nearly nude girl, now passed out from shock, up the alley and into an abandoned warehouse nearby.

She was about twenty, with long, wavy, brunette hair, ivory smooth skin, and a taut, curvaceous figure that was now bruised and sullied with street grime and bodily fluids, little of which were her own. She also had track marks on her arm, but he didn't know what they were.

Despite the experiments, human beings were still an alien species to him.

The big man set her down gently on the dusty floor. He hadn't even had a chance to finish his first meal in two days, having dropped the tuna during the struggle. But he didn't care. At least he wasn't alone anymore.

As he sat beside her, contemplating her broken beauty with sadness, his mind wandered back to his place of origin, his memories as murky as the lagoon that spawned him, so many, many years ago, and so very, very far away from here…

She reminded him of the girl he'd first seen swimming along the surface of the Amazon River as he glided deep below her on a parallel path. Even though his brain had been chemically altered, he recalled her angelic visage, and the primitively erotic sensation of her soft skin against his scales, which had been shed due to the scientifically engineered transformation, forcibly induced while he was in captivity for the second time.

Why couldn't they have just let him alone?

The expedition that first disrupted his tranquil, solitary existence in his natural habitat was not the first. They left him for dead. The second, commissioned by an aquarium in Florida, drugged and kidnapped him from his home and put him on public display as a source of amusement for gawking tourists, chained and humiliated, his resistance kept in check by an electronic prod.

Until he escaped, and wreaked havoc in this civilized society until he was again shot, and mistaken for deceased.

The third time he was discovered and held captive was by a team of scientists that transported him from the Florida Everglades to the San Francisco Bay Area, where he was caged at a private Marin County residence after operations that removed much of his original identity, converting him from a humanoid amphibian to something closer to a human being, essentially manipulating the process of evolution by accelerating a mutation that might've otherwise taken centuries.

Once again, he escaped captivity, wounded and near death, returning to the only sanctuary he knew: the nearest large body of water, which happened to be the Pacific Ocean.

But his gunshot wounds, along with the fact his gills had been surgically removed, disallowing his ability to breathe underwater, much less in unfamiliar saltwater, would've proven fatal had the sole passenger of a passing yacht not found him floundering near the shore, gasping for air.

The boat's occupant, a retired medical doctor on vacation, rescued the drowning mutant, and assumed he was either a disfigured burn victim or a poor soul suffering from a progressively degenerative disease, like acromegaly.

The doctor treated the mutant's wounds and fed him life-saving nutrients intravenously. The mutant was touched by the doctor's kindness since it was an unprecedented attribute in his experience with humans thus far.

By the time the yacht returned to its homeport off Bainbridge Island, just across Puget Sound from Seattle, the doctor and the mutant had become friends, communicating only with hand gestures.

Two years later, the doctor and the mutant, now dubbed "Phinn," after the doctor's late wife's maiden name, were close friends, though no one knew of this secret relationship. Phinn was kept hidden away in the doctor's remote residence, where he was taught the English language and some rudimentary skills of social function.

The doctor even showed him 16mm newsreels to inform him about the outside world and provide context for his other lessons, conducted with the aid of books, which Phinn gradually learned to read.

Unintentionally, the doctor succeeded in expediting the manufactured evolutionary process that had begun on that boat from Florida. But Phinn accepted his fate and was grateful for the companionship and sanctuary.

Then one day the doctor died suddenly of a heart attack while they were sharing a meal in the dining room. Phinn was confused and devastated. Grief-stricken, he wandered out into the night.

Though he knew he could no longer swim underwater due to his altered physique, Phinn realized he could still swim above the surface. Given his immense strength and stamina, he was able to cross Puget Sound and come ashore on a secluded section of the harbor.

Phinn rolled a bum sleeping in an alley for his pants, and when a terrified, well-dressed businessman caught sight of him at dawn, Phinn grabbed him, removed his hat and coat, and then let him go. His urge to kill had greatly diminished over the past two years.

But his primitive instincts had not been completely mollified by the hormonal injections.

After hiding out in the shadows of society for two days, Phinn decided to try roaming amongst the humans in his "disguise," driven by hunger.

The girl woke up suddenly, saw Phinn's face, and screamed. A tear rolled down one of his greenish cheeks. Tear ducts were one of several involuntarily triggered biological by-products of the transformation that still surprised him.

But then she stopped after sitting up and assessing the situation. Phinn had found some old newspapers and covered her exposed flesh with a makeshift blanket.

"Who are you?" she asked in a hoarse whisper.

"I am…Phinn," he responded in his halting, gravelly voice, still adjusting to the development of biologically synthesized vocal cords. "I…saved you from…the…the…"

"Thank you," she said as tears escaped her eyes as well. "Thank you. My name is Julie."

Phinn nodded, then bowed his head, no longer able to sustain direct facial contact, suddenly ashamed of his wretched countenance.

Julie reached out with a trembling hand and wiped the tear from his cheek. "You saved me. No one else has ever done that for me before. Ever."

"Someone saved me…once," Phinn said, his normally slow speech pattern accelerating with emotional momentum. "So now…I save you. Can you also save me? I need…to hide…"

"What's wrong with you?" Julie asked abruptly, letting her internal thoughts slip through her restrained façade. Despite her gratitude, she found Phinn's appearance unsettling. But she didn't want to alienate her savior with an outward expression of revulsion. So she instantly recalibrated her reaction, and said, "I mean…are you sick or something?"

"I'm…just…this is just who I am," he said. "I am sorry. Should I leave you now?"

"No!" Julie said, grabbing hold of his cold hand. "Please. Come with me. I live not too far from here."

Standing up and wobbling a bit from the effort, Julie, still holding Phinn's hand, gestured for him to rise with her. The newspapers all fell away from her body, exposing her breasts.

Phinn removed his trench coat and put it around her, even though that meant revealing his misshapen torso.

Julie reached out and touched one of his bulging pectoral muscles. "You are so strong," she said in a whisper.

Phinn nodded humbly. "We should be careful, so no one sees me…like this."

"I will protect you," Julie said, leading him out of the warehouse and back into the alley, then quickly through the few throngs of pedestrians toward her apartment a few blocks away. Phinn kept the Fedora over his face, shielding the most alarming aspect of his appearance.

Her studio apartment was sparsely furnished,

equipped with a kitchenette, a tiny bathroom, and a Murphy bed she usually kept pulled out, since it was where she spent much of her time, working for Frank.

In fact, the boys that had raped her were initially "customers," but when she rejected a gang-bang, even for cash, they decided to make it a gang rape, without charge. They had chased her out of the apartment and to that alley, where she met Phinn.

She considered it kismet, despite the expense of her pride.

"I'm sorry I can't offer you someplace more comfortable," Julie said.

"I am very comfortable," Phinn said, smiling inwardly since his mouth retained too much of its original composition for him to actually do so.

She pulled up one of the wooden chairs from her Formica dining table—the only other piece of furniture in the room—and sat on it while offering the bed to Phinn.

"You'd only break the chair," she said with a grin.

Phinn agreed and sat on the edge of the bed, which creaked under his weight.

"Where do you come from?" she asked.

"That is a long story," he said.

"I have time now," she replied. "I don't have to go to work until late tonight."

So he told her everything. And she accepted it.

Then she told him all about her.

"I ran away from home when I was only sixteen," she said. "So I know what it's like to be homeless, like you. My father was…like Frank. He treated me like Frank treats me. Even…you know. I loved my mother, but she died a long time ago. So finally I couldn't take it anymore, so I ran away. I'd rather be alone than living with a monster. Oh, I'm sorry."

"I understand," Phinn said. "Please continue."

"Well, Frank found me one night and at first he was very kind. He offered me food and shelter and a job dancing in his club. And that's all I did, at first. Then at a party upstairs one night he asked me if I wanted to try some, you know, drugs, and I was already drunk so I did, and next thing I know, I was under his thumb. He made me do other things too, that I don't want to talk about. I've been thinking I need to get away now. Maybe…maybe we can go away together. I've been thinking of escaping to the San Juan Islands, up north, and hiding away in a cabin in the woods that my mother once owned. My father never goes there anymore, but if he did…well, I have you now, don't I?"

Phinn nodded.

"I've made up my mind," she said.

The Naughty Nautical's blue neon sign—shaped like a mermaid—beamed through the darkness and light rain as Phinn and Julie cautiously approached the nightclub's rear entrance and entered discreetly.

The place was dark and rather small, decorated with tiki statues and other "exotic" décor, including dangling fishnets and fish float lamps.

A West Coast Jazz quartet was performing on stage in between the burlesque acts, the saxophone player and drummer always staying to provide backup music for the dancers while the guitar player and flutist took a break. The owner, a local gangster named Frank, was behind the bar. He was also a pimp and drug dealer. Taking full advantage of her gullibility and vulnerability, he got Julie hooked on heroin when she was only seventeen, three years earlier. Then he forced her to work the streets.

Now all that was about to change, Julie decided. The rape, as physically abusive and psychologically traumatic as it had been, finally gave her the inner strength to stand up to her male oppressors, especially now that she had Phinn for both emotional and physical support.

Phinn was now accustomed to walking quickly with the hat over his face, so they made their way past a few patrons sitting at tables watching the voluptuous dancer that had just taken the stage, up the dark stairs, and to Frank's office.

"Wait for me here," Julie said after she let Phinn inside. He nodded.

Then she went back downstairs and to the bar, where she confronted Frank, who was sipping a Martini he had made himself. The regular bartender he had been relieving had just clocked back in.

"Hey, you're up next!" Frank said menacingly to Julie. "Get into costume, so you can get back out of it!"

He was a large man, though not nearly as large as Phinn, with slick black hair and a rotund physique. He had greasy, pockmarked facial flesh and cold eyes as dark as coal. He seemed to be perpetually drooling from the left side of his mouth. Everything about him disgusted her, and yet she had allowed him to make love to her several times, in exchange for the drugs. But never again.

"I'm quitting," she said resolutely. "We can talk about this in your office. I want my pay, then I'm gone. For good."

He laughed at first but then stopped when he realized she was serious. "You know what this means?" he said, pantomiming a hypodermic needle shot into the right sleeve of his shiny silk suit.

"I'm done with that too," she said. "All of it. Let's go."

The eavesdropping bartender tried suppressing his amusement, but when Frank began chuckling, they both shared a laugh.

"Sure toots," Frank said. "Let's go upstairs and work this out…" He then winked at the bartender as he followed Julie back to his office.

There Phinn was standing behind the desk, waiting. He bristled as they entered. Frank's jaw was agape.

"Who the hell are you?" he demanded.

"This is my friend, Phinn," Julie said confidently. "I brought him along to make sure you don't try any funny business. Not that I'm joking, either. Now give me my money, we'll leave, and you'll never see us again."

"'Zat so?" Frank said, his gaze still deadlocked with Phinn's.

"Yes," Julie responded resolutely.

Phinn's intimidating presence finally won the brief showdown. Frank went to the wall safe, spun the knob, opened it, and removed a stack of bills, tossing it at Julie with condescending contempt.

"Take your pet monster and get the hell out of my sight," Frank said.

With a triumphant smile, Julie nodded, gestured at Phinn, and they both left.

Back at her apartment, Julie celebrated by making Phinn a seafood dinner and drinks. She mixed her own

Mai Tai's, using the original recipe she learned from one of the bartenders at the nightclub, and they sat listening to her transistor radio for a while, without speaking. Phinn had often consumed wine and bourbon when living with the doctor, so alcohol was not an unfamiliar substance. He rather enjoyed its intoxicating effects.

Finally, as Bobby Darin was singing "Dream Lover," Julie stood up, went over to Phinn, kissed him passionately on the lips, and then he lifted her and carried her to her bed, following his own primeval mating instincts.

After they made love, Phinn held Julie in his arms and fell asleep, dreaming of a lonely, prehistoric place that was growing dimmer and dimmer in his memory. He had never known such peace.

She made him breakfast the next morning, a shrimp and crab omelet that he consumed with rare relish, and they sat and talked about their future together, perhaps in the San Juan Islands, or even further north.

"Have you ever been to Vancouver?" she asked. "Oh wait, of course not. My mother is from there and took me there to visit her parents when I was just a child. We grew up in Tacoma, which is not far from here. Anyway, Vancouver is very nice too, but there are a lot of people there, and it's cold. You probably prefer someplace warm and tropical, right?"

Phinn shrugged. "Anyplace with you will be…paradise," he said.

She smiled and said, "Maybe Hawaii! It's going to be an official state soon!"

For once, the possibilities seemed limitless. She could relate so much to Phinn's isolation from the rest of her own race. She had always felt like she belonged to a different species, undefined, but distinct from everyone else she ever knew. Until now.

Later that evening she took him to a drive-in where they watched a double bill: Elvis Presley's latest movie, his last before being inducted into the Army, entitled *King Creole*, plus the new sci-fi hit *I Married a Monster from Outer Space*, though they didn't really pay much attention to either one. They were too distracted by their newfound freedom and friendship.

When they got home, Julie was obviously ill, going through severe withdrawals after quitting her addiction so suddenly. She writhed on the floor, sweating and coughing and crying, finally vomiting in the kitchen sink.

Phinn held her in his arms as they lay in bed together, and she finally fell asleep. Hours passed this way.

Then the door to her apartment burst open and there was Frank, his worst suspicions confirmed. Beside him were two henchmen who grabbed Julie while training their guns on Phinn.

"I'll take care of you later, freak," Frank said as he yanked Julie by the hair.

Phinn assumed they had gone back to the nightclub, so he returned there. Two men were guarding the door. Phinn quickly disposed of them, fatally but quietly, before heading up to Frank's office.

Phinn arrived just in time to see Frank sitting on top of her as he pummeled her face with his fists. Phinn rushed Frank and quickly subdued him.

Lifting Frank high above his head, Phinn threw the gangster through the window, spectacularly smashing the panes. Frank was propelled with brutal force down into the alley below, where his screaming body bounced off of a fire escape before landing with a loud thud on the edge of an open garbage dumpster, then falling to the wet ground like a broken doll.

Phinn turned to see Julie lying dead on the ground. He had been too late to save her. Frank had beaten her badly. After Phinn kneeled and lifted her, she dangled limp and lifeless in Phinn's powerful arms. He wept for a moment, then roared and set her down gently on the floor.

Phinn rampaged through the nightclub, ripping chairs, tables, and bodies into pieces. Blood splattered, bones and wood splintered, bottles of booze shattered.

Frank's two henchmen opened fire with machine guns, riddling Phinn's body with bullets. The barrage slowed him down but did not stop him. He ran toward them and ripped each of their heads off, keeping both of his slightly webbed hands busy, tossing their decapitated craniums aside like softballs.

Wracked with pain and weak from blood loss, Phinn staggered out into the night, heading towards the Sound and its soothing waves.

He was almost about to wade into the water and let himself drown this time. But then he remembered Julie's face, her touch, the short ray of hope she had given him, and the alleviation of his lifelong loneliness, if only briefly.

This image of her smile made him stop short. Life was worthing enduring if only for this one sweet moment indelibly enshrined in his memory. He decided he'd try to swim along the surface, despite his badly leaking torso, north to the San Juan Islands, the place his Julie had considered as a possible future home for them both.

Now he'd just live there alone, like he was back in the lagoon. At least no one could hurt him anymore.

But then a honking sound followed by wild whooping noises broke the somber contemplation of his immediate options.

The truck pulling up fast behind him was full of the same delinquents that had gang-raped Julie. Phinn recognized them right away, but in his weakened state, he was in no position to fight them again. As the truck came to a stop directly in front of him, the radio was blaring "Be-Bop-a-Lula" by Gene Vincent.

The four teenage thugs jumped out of the truck and surrounded Phinn, brandishing bats and chains, only a few feet from the Sound's shore and his freedom. They had been driving around looking for him ever since that night, ready to dole out violent vengeance.

In the darkness of the alley they never really had a good look at him. Now that he was exposed in the moonlight, they were both shocked and amused.

"Look at them fat lips!"

"And them little beady eyes!"

"And that bald monkey head!"

"He ain't nothin' but a bleached nigger, all right!"

Phinn was passive as they beat him down to the ground, then tied him up with rope and threw him in the back of the truck.

They drove him to a remote corner of Lake Washington in Magnusson Park. There they dragged him out of the truck and threw him on the ground beneath a large tree next to the water. They used the rope that entangled Phinn to string him up on one of the stronger branches, and a crate from the back of the truck to keep him stable, for the time being.

"Any last words, nigger?" the leader of the mob asked Phinn.

After a pause, Phinn said, "It was not my choice to be brought here to walk among you. I meant you no harm. I only wished to assimilate and be left alone to live my own life, in peace. Now you choose to destroy me. Why?"

The mob stared back at him in silence. "Endless Sleep" by Jody Reynolds was blasting from the truck's radio.

Then the leader grinned and kicked the crate out from under Phinn's formerly webbed feet. He could no longer swim against the tide of his own fate.

(Originally published in *Pop the Clutch: Thrilling Tales of Rockabilly, Monsters, and Hot Rod Horror*, Dark Moon Press, 2019.)

LIVING PROOF

A Vic Valentine Vignette

As we grow older and closer to our unknown individual expiration date, every extra day of life feels like a stay of execution. But everyone's death sentence is passed the day we're born, uniformly upheld without any exact dates for us to plan around, and we can only evade the inevitable for so long. I'd been hired to find out why some guy had died clear across the country. But the thing is, the reason we all die ultimately doesn't matter, because sooner or later, it finds us, whoever and wherever we are. Some sooner than others, of course. Whether luck of the draw or Fate, it's totally irrelevant. I wasn't ready to go yet, but then as I said, Death doesn't share its appointment calendar with anyone in advance.

South Carolina, my unlikely destination in this particular case, was never a state I thought I'd wind up in. State of depression, state of confusion, state of decay, sure. But South Carolina just never made my travel radar, any more than North Carolina or North Dakota or South Dakota for that matter. They just seemed like places cut in two that could've just as easily remained as one, but then you could say that about a lot of things, like sandwiches or marriages. Then again, maybe not.

The place where I was told I could get some information was a cozy little joint called the Yonder Southern Cocktails and Brew. I was instructed by my mysterious client to ask for the owner, whose name was Eryk, spelled with a 'y' for some reason. Apparently, that aberration didn't affect the pronunciation, so it didn't matter. Not to me, anyway.

"I'm looking for Eryk with a 'y'," I said to the guy behind the bar as I took a seat. He was a clean-cut dude with an organically friendly manner, which made me immediately suspicious, but then I was raised in Brooklyn.

He smiled quizzically. "Eryk. With a 'y'."

"Yeah."

"You mean, like, with a question?"

"Several."

"I have one first. Why do you want to see him?"

"For some answers."

"What makes you think he has them?"

"I don't. Only way to find out is to ask."

"Well, you found him."

"You're Eryk? With a 'y'?"

"Yeah. Who are you?"

"Vic Valentine. I'm a dick from San Francisco."

"I hear there's loads of 'em back there."

"Well, I'm the biggest." That didn't come out right or maybe it did. I'm not as adept at self-assessment anymore than I am at self-censorship.

"You must be good," he said.

"Why?"

"Exactly."

"I mean, good at what?"

"You're a detective and you already found who you're looking for."

"Well, I was told to ask for you here, so I kinda had a head start."

"Who told you to ask for me?"

"I can't tell you that." The reason was that I didn't really know.

"Well, then I can't tell you anything, either. Guy like you walks in out of the blue, what am I supposed to do? You could be a hitman for all I know."

"I look like a hitman to you?"

"A short one."

"Short? What, like Joe Pesci?"

He laughed. "I'm just giving you a hard time. What's with the suit and tie? Aren't you hot?"

I loosened my skinny tie a bit. My shiny Sharkskin suit did stand out amid all the T-shirts and shorts and sandals surrounding me, but then I was a walking anachronism wherever I went. I looked back at the few patrons, sitting around the tables talking about politics and sports, subjects I always avoided, along with religion and why it feels so good to wipe your own ass. A couple of them gave me the once-over, but not in a menacing or patronizing way. Just passively curious. I avoided eye contact, as I always do. I don't like people and the feeling is generally mutual. "Yeah, well, I have to keep up appearances," I finally said in response.

"Is this snazzy old outfit, like, your uniform?"

"Kinda."

"I always wondered how Jack Lord did it."

"Did what?"

"Wore a suit all the time. In Hawaii."

He won me over with that reference. "Yeah, me too. Speaking of which, any good tiki bars around here?"

"Is that the question you wanted to ask me?"

"No."

"Well, good, because there ain't. Not that I know

of. I can make you a Mai Tai if you want."

"The original one with lime juice and orgeat or the touristy one with grenadine and pineapple juice?"

He gave me a funny look, which meant I just ordered a Manhattan.

"Okay, I can make you that. We got premium bourbon. Any particular preference?"

"Bartender's choice."

He just nodded and said, "But unless you tell me why you're here, I'm not answering any questions."

"I'm actually looking for a dead guy."

"I can't make you a Zombie either."

"No, I meant, not his corpse. Just wondering what happened to him, or rather how it happened. I'm told you knew him."

Eryk seemed to ponder the question as he took out his cell phone from a back pocket. At first, I was worried he was Googling "How to Make a Manhattan," which was as Basic Mixology 101 as the bottle of Wild Turkey he had pulled down from the shelf behind him. Turned out he was just sending a text, or so it seemed. Then he quietly poured the hard booze into a shaker, added the proper amount of sweet vermouth with some bitters, shook it up, and served it to me, up and perfectly chilled. He'd even garnished it with the right type of cherry, too. I took a sip, letting him think it over. The drink was damn good.

"Without you even telling me, I know who you mean," he said finally.

"Okay. So?"

"So some people are coming over here soon who can help you out."

"Wow. Well, thanks."

"Don't mention it." Suddenly his demeanor was as icy as my cocktail, but I didn't care. He went about his business, and I just stared at the backlit bar, idly dreaming about Bettie Page because that's what I always do when I'm bored. And even when I'm not.

An indeterminate amount of time passed before two people sidled up on either side of me, taking their seats with a sense of secret purpose. I knew they were there to see me. Eryk came over to greet them.

"Marietta," he said to the attractive woman on my left.

"Eryk," she said.

"Shawn," he said to the big badass on my right.

"Eryk," he said with a nod.

"Sean?" I said. "As in Sean Connery?"

"More like Idris Elba," the big guy said.

"Hey, I got nothing against a black Bond." I was already making a fool of myself. Why waste time, I figured. It was going to happen eventually.

"I spell my name differently," he said without missing a beat.

"Than Idris Elba? I can't even spell *his*."

He shook his head slowly, waiting for me to catch up.

"Oh. *Sean*. How else can you spell it?"

"Think about it."

I did as I was told. Then it hit me. "Oh! Like Shaun of the Dead."

"Nope."

I thought about it some more. Then I said, "Oh, like Prawn?"

He turned his head and looked me dead in the eyes. Suddenly I had to pee. "I look like a damn prawn to you?"

I shook my head, and then he laughed and slapped me on the back, making me spit out some of my drink. I tried to laugh too, but only drooled. I was embarrassing myself at a record clip, even for me.

I turned to the woman, hoping for a smooth transition back to Coolsville. No dice. She was staring at the boozy saliva dripping from my lips. She handed me a napkin. I wiped my mouth and said, "Marietta, yes?"

"Sometimes," she said.

"Not your real name?"

"Why would I tell you if it wasn't? Wouldn't that ruin the whole idea of having an alias?"

"Good point."

"These folks know the guy you're looking for," Eryk said, coming to my rescue, probably to expedite the conversation so we could all just move on with our lives already. At least that was my motivation.

Feeling intimidated, I said, "Well, I was only told to ask for you."

"You did. And then I asked for my friends here."

That's when both Marietta and Shawn took out their guns and put them on the bar in front of them. Two .45 Colts. Eryk didn't even flinch.

"I didn't know this was an open carry state," I said nervously.

"It's not," Shawn said. "They were concealed first."

"Oh. You a cop?"

"No. I work in a mortuary."

"So you *are* like Shaun of the Dead."

"Ha ha ha," he said without a trace of amusement. "Haven't heard that one before."

"Guy you're talking about?" Marietta chimed in. "Last time we saw him, he wasn't dead."

"So maybe he died since then," I said.

"I would've noticed," Shawn said. "He's not a customer of mine. Not yet."

"Maybe we're not talking about the same guy," I said.

"Yes, you are," Eryk said.

"How do you know?"

"Because I'm the guy who hired you."

I'd only had one drink, and not even all of it yet, so I couldn't blame my confusion on alcohol, my usual alibi. "You hired me to come out here and find you?"

"Not find me. Ask for me."

"How can this be?"

"Think about it. All you got was a phone call and a wire transfer into your account. You never met me. Until now."

"Why all the subterfuge? And why not just hire someone local?"

"Because we don't want anyone knowing about this. No one around here."

"How did you pick me?"

"Phone book."

"But why me?"

"You're cheap. All I could afford. Plus you agreed to fly out here on your own dime."

"I was figuring you'd reimburse me."

"I'm not. That was included in the fee."

"Aw, shit." I downed the rest of my drink, got up from the stool, and was ready to walk out when Shawn stood up and blocked me, overshadowing me like a total eclipse. I sat back down.

"I don't get it," I said. "But then I don't really get anything."

"You're forgetting something else," Eryk said.

"I've always had a bad memory, at least as I recall."

"I thought you were a detective," Shawn said. "Eye for detail, all that."

"Not really. The only reason I can even remember to jerk off every day is muscle memory."

"TMI," Marietta said.

"Sorry, sometimes I forget myself in the company of ladies."

"You always this crude?" she asked.

"When I was young and stupid."

"What are you now?"

"A lot less young, a little less stupid."

"But still crude."

"I try to be polite. It's not a hard and fast rule."

"I got your hard and fast rule right here," Shawn said. "More like a hard and fast ruler. All twelve inches."

"Hey, a lady is present," I said.

Both Shawn and Marietta laughed again. Eryk didn't. He just kept staring at me, waiting for me to figure out why I was there.

"I'm getting the idea you flew me out here just to mess with me," I said. "Hey, you paid me. Knock yourselves out."

"We want you to kill him," Eryk said flatly.

I was carrying a .38. I hadn't pulled it yet because, for one thing, I was outgunned. They obviously anticipated the fact I was strapped, given my so-called profession. But I wasn't a contract killer by any stretch.

"I thought I was too short to be a hitman," I said.

"Tall enough," Shawn said. "Just aim up."

"What makes you think I would kill someone?"

"Because if you don't, we'll kill you," Marietta said.

"And nobody will miss you," Shawn said. "Even if they did, like your friend Doc out there, they wouldn't be able to find you. See, we offer cremation services at my place of business."

"So it would be like the end of 'Ocean's Eleven'," I said, trying to inject some levity into the suddenly serious proceedings with a random retro-reference.

"What are you talking about?" Marietta asked.

"He means the original," Eryk said. "The old one. With the Rat Pack."

"I never even heard of it," Marietta said.

"Because it sucks," Shawn said.

"Well, you're just going to have to kill me," I said. "I don't even like eating meat. In fact, I'm thinking of becoming a vegan."

"So you don't dig barbecue," Shawn said.

"No, which is why this whole cremating scenario doesn't work for me, either. When I get my ashes hauled, I'm thinking of something else entirely."

"You think we won't kill you?" Eryk said.

"No. For one thing, you have too many witnesses." I gestured behind me to the patrons at the tables, who suddenly had their guns out, too, aimed right at me. It was all a set-up. I felt like I was trapped in a remake of *Two Thousand Maniacs* (1964), except that had already been remade in 2005 as *2001 Maniacs*. Not bad, actually. Still, I didn't want to star in the documentary version.

"What was it I forgot again?" I said.

"When we talked on the phone," Eryk said. "I told you not to book a return flight."

"I thought that was because you'd book it for me."

"He's not," Shawn and Marietta both said in unison. Everyone in the damn bar kept their guns trained on me. I looked yearningly at the door. That's when one of the patrons got up and locked it.

So this was it. I was either going to kill someone or get killed myself. Shawn had mentioned my friend Doc back in San Francisco, the only person who really gave a damn about me. They'd done their research. But good. They were right. I didn't really have any friends or family to speak of. No lovers, none that would notice I was suddenly gone, anyway. Maybe my friend Monica. She was a waitress back at Doc's joint, The Drive-Inn. But she'd get over me. I hadn't told her or Doc where I was going, because that was part of the initial instructions. Now I knew why. Eventually, the cops would find out I'd bought a one-way ticket to South Carolina. But then the trail would go cold. My dusty remains would get flushed down the toilet and that would be that.

"Okay, just do it," I said. "I don't care."

They all looked at me. "What do you mean, you don't care?" Eryk said.

"Kill me. I got nothing to live for. But do it quick. Find some other sucker."

"I'll just beat you till you agree," Shawn said.

"Go ahead. I'm a glutton for punishment. Ask any of my ex-girlfriends."

"We did," Marietta said. "Including Monica."

"Shit. Did you threaten her?"

"No man," Shawn said. "I called the Drive-Inn and

asked for you. She answered. I just told her I was a potential client, asked a few questions, got a few answers, and hung up. She had no idea why. But we know who she is, and where she lives. Doc, too. Now you ready to cooperate or not? Because here's the thing: either way, you're gonna burn."

"That sucks," I said. "I hate the heat. That's why I'm thinking of moving to Seattle."

"Ain't gonna happen," Shawn said.

I really hated heat more than anything, so that settled it. Fuck the other guy, whoever he was. "Okay, who do you want me to ice, and why?" I said with resignation.

They all looked at each other, then back at me, and broke into laughter.

"Me," Eryk said. "I want you to kill me."

Then everyone stopped laughing, while I was just getting started. But he was dead serious, or so it seemed.

"This just keeps getting weirder," I said. "But then Life is like that. Mine, anyway."

"Just kidding!" Eryk said. Everyone laughed again. "See, we're not criminals. Just crime writers. We're working on an anthology of stories, and we were stuck on a unifying theme. So we pooled our money, searched the Internet, found a sucker, and flew him— meaning you—out here, set up this situation, and took bets on what you'd do, how you'd react to the ultimatum. On top of being a creative project, it was an experiment in human nature."

"And I'm the guinea pig."

"We'll make it up to you, promise!" Marietta said.

"Like how?"

"You like to drink, right?"

"You really have done your homework."

Shawn then pointed his gun between my eyes and said, "First shot on me." Then he pulled the trigger and blasted me right in the face. It was a water pistol, loaded with whiskey.

Then they all started laughing. Again. At my expense. Literally. I still had to buy my own return ticket to San Francisco. Meantime, as compensation for my time and effort, I was allowed to drink and eat the equivalent, on the house. Marietta hooked me up with a room to stay for a few days, where I was provided with some rather alarming accommodations.

"I heard all you think about is sex," she said to me as she drove me to the rather remote property on the edge of town.

"Heard from who?"

"Word gets around cyberspace."

"So you're virtually stalking me."

"I'd call it research for our project. So is it true? You're obsessed with sex?"

"I guess. What else is there, really? I mean, sure, there are other things. But who cares? What else am I going to think about? Death?"

"Life's brevity is what gives it meaning," she said. "It would be meaningless to live forever."

"But isn't sex where life comes from? I'm just acknowledging our own origins. On a semi-regular basis."

"Who is your ideal woman?"

"Jessica Rabbit."

"She doesn't actually exist."

"Exactly. It's my excuse for not being married."

She just smiled and kept driving while I kept quiet.

Though the town had its share of attractions, none of which appealed to me much, I hardly ever left the sparsely furnished room, which was upstairs inside a dilapidated, dank, dusty old mansion that had been long abandoned, with moss-covered walls painted puke green like it was Poison Ivy's lair, intimidatingly misshapen shadows, fully occupied cobwebs, and almost impenetrably grimy mirrors with ornate frames that seemed like gateways to Hell. Except it felt like I was already on that side of the looking glass, only with forbidden pleasures as my eternal compensation. I was okay with that deal.

Due to my checkered history with sordid people in seedy environments, I feel perfectly comfortable when slightly in danger. This place was like many of the scary places I'd stayed in my life, residential hotels and such, purely out of poverty and desperation. But this one was different, because of the gratuitous rewards for simply showing up. On top of my generous and open-ended bar tab, everyone at Yonder bought me drinks. Many drinks. And food. I chose mostly plant-based stuff, in anticipation of my potential dietary tweaks. And by "plant-based" I mean french fries and extra olives for my Martinis, since this was the Deep South, after all, though the chef made some mean collard greens to go with my black-eyed peas a couple of times. Essentially, though, I happily subsisted on gin salads all week.

These strange, friendly folks had my number, all right. It was both unsettling and welcome.

Especially when Marietta introduced me to the main reason I hardly ever left the scary room in the scary house: a local friend of hers who looked and even dressed (and undressed) like Tina Louise in *God's Little Acre* (1958), at least through my desperately cinematic lens. Tina's profession was made apparent right away, before I met her, and I had no problem with it, especially since I wasn't footing the bill for her services. She provided me with carnal company every night and day, all on the bar's expense account, though I got the impression Tina was taking it out in trade, booze-wise. Fine with me, since I was the beneficiary. And I didn't even have to kill anyone for it. Though in her case, I'd have certainly considered it.

Then things got even weirder, and I was back in my comfort zone.

I won't divulge any salacious details of our tryst out of respect for Tina, as I called her, since she made me promise to keep everything we did a secret and not to divulge her real name to anyone since I obviously had no shame, but she did, though she certainly didn't act like it when alone with me. Maybe she was just embarrassed to be screwing a Left Coast loser. All I'll say is those Southern belles know how to ring-a-ding-ding. In my nightly post-coital stupor, I slept more soundly than I had in years, except when I was awakened by what sounded like muffled chainsaws and screams I occasionally heard from deep down in "the cellar." Initially, I thought they were nightmares that rudely wake you up and make you wonder if you're still dreaming. But I'm always dreaming, so I can't tell anymore.

When I mentioned this to Tina, she denied it and told me I was hearing things, and I said yes, that's the problem. When it got to the point where it was undeniable, especially when we both put our ears to the locked, steel cellar door, and nobody responded when I pounded on it, she simply shrugged and turned up the volume of her vintage CD boom box, which perpetually played only one song on repeat from the *Pulp Fiction* soundtrack, "If Love is a Red Dress," by Maria McKee, whom I knew as the lead singer of an L.A. band from the 80s called Lone Justice. Tina claimed she never heard of that band or any other song by Maria McKee, since "If Love is a Red Dress" was her favorite song and the only song she ever listened to, even during sex. Especially during sex. To this day, I get an erection whenever I hear it. Of course, that was true before I ever met Tina.

It didn't bother me because I really like that song, that singer, and that movie, though if I were to pick a song to put on perpetual repeat, and since I can't pick just one, it would be "Lujon" blended with "Peter Gunn," both by Henry Mancini. At least that combo sort of fits. Alternates include "Rebel Yell" by Billy Idol in a mashup with "I'm Gonna Live Till I Die" by Frank Sinatra. Or "Cry Me a River" by Julie London mixed with "Call Me" by Blondie. Don't ask me why. I guess I'm just a conflicted kind of guy.

Finally, when I took the CD out of the boom box and held it hostage, Tina told me that the cellar was a butcher's residence and he often catered to clients with his personally curated barnyard stock, which seemed odd, because there was no barn on the property, and the screams, however hard to hear clearly, sounded human, not swine or bovine. Anyway, this experience was eventually part of what made me finally decide to go full vegan, at least on this trip, especially when Tina told me the butcher was her husband.

I happened to catch one brief glimpse of him as he was heading down into the cellar one day. His face was stern, swarthy, and pock-marked, his big body both fat and muscular, with a hairy chest and back but a balding cranium, completely coated in slimy sweat. Additionally, he was heavily tattooed with demonic and patriotic symbols, wearing a blood-stained wife-beater, soiled dark pants, and muddy, black work shoes. He was actually carrying a hatchet. Even from across the living room, he smelled like Carnal Death. (As a semi-professional or at least self-delusional detective, I've learned to notice and memorize these kinds of details, all the time, as a survival mechanism.) The Butcher seemed to quickly meet my gaze and smirk just before he slammed and locked the cellar door behind him. Maybe I just hallucinated that, since I was momentarily petrified with dread. It didn't matter.

When Tina came back to the mansion loaded up with potato chips and booze for our dinner, I asked if her "husband" approved of her profession, since she clearly had no problems with his, and more urgently, if he knew I was a client, not some distant cousin she was temporarily entertaining, though maybe that wouldn't have made a difference around here. She casually explained he was perfectly fine with any way she "brought home the bacon," even though I figured they made their own, homegrown and freshly killed.

Deep in a white trash sex haze, I managed to simply block out all potentially problematic possibilities, like the Butcher hacking my back with an axe while I was on top of his wife. The sex was worth the risk, but I remained distractingly paranoid about possibly winding up on a hillbilly cannibal menu that was tacked to the greasy wall of an informal slaughterhouse. Meaning the one I was in. I had no problem with the private torture chamber as long as he wasn't harming animals, but from what I heard, which vaguely sounded like a baby in a blender with a blanket over it, that was not the case, making it even harder to ignore.

On our final night together, and possibly my final night, period, Tina had a confession for me. Since the moment we met, she seemed stoic and lost, her smoldering sensuality shrouded and smothered in sadness, which slowly suffocated me, too. And because of her soft, curvy flesh, I let it.

"That butcher," she whispered ominously in the dark, after a particularly kinky evening.

"Your husband?"

"Yeah."

"What about him?"

"He's not really a butcher."

"So he isn't killing animals?"

"No."

"What about the screams?"

"I said no animals. What difference does it make?"

"Because I actually like animals. All of them. Well, most of them. Maybe not mosquitoes lately. It's a sliding scale."

"You're sliding on your own shit."

"Ok. So then the screams must be human unless he's chopping up sentient cauliflower?"

"I can't tell you anything else."

"Then why did you even bring it up?"

"I thought that's why I was here," she said, tugging my tuckered-out pecker.

"You know what I mean."

"So you wouldn't be scared."

"Who said I was scared?"

"Your dick."

"Not always. It's just resting between rounds like an aged-out boxer too proud to quit."

"Well enough so that I had to say something."

"I wasn't scared, just so you know. But for the record, he is a butcher, of some sort. Admit that, at least."

She paused, then finally said, "Yes."

"Should I be worried, if not scared?"

"*No*, he already knows we're fucking. What do you think he is, an idiot? In fact, he's watching us right now."

I shot straight up in bed as my boner wilted like a daisy in a wildfire. "*What*? He's *here*?"

"No, there's a hidden camera. He watches from the cellar."

"Um, I don't know how I feel about this."

"Well, if you don't like it, we'll just stop screwing and I'll leave. I've fulfilled my obligation, anyway."

"*No*! No, that's okay. I just hope he's not taping it or anything. I have a reputation to protect."

She laughed for the only time in my presence but didn't deny it.

"What happens in this town stays in this town," she finally said. "You know, like Vegas. That's why you must never tell anyone anything about what we did here."

"It's not what *we* did that's bothering me."

Her brain radio abruptly went silent and I stopped frantically station-surfing. I really didn't want to know any more details because I had a feeling further revelations would spoil rather than simply strain the romantic mood.

But I kept scanning the room for the alleged hidden camera as Tina the Butcher's Wife blew me to smithereens. I decided it just had to be inside the depressingly eerie deer head mounted on the opposite wall, staring at my shameless sins with cold, glassy eyes that seemed to say, "I didn't do anything to deserve this. And neither will you." The sad truth is the voyeuristic scenario she described actually turned me on. Well, a little. Enough to keep it up long enough before it naturally went back down, anyway.

Despite the raw, savage, cathartic if psychologically complex sex, I was ready to get the hell out of there.

On my sixth and final morning there, I couldn't find Tina anywhere in the house. I heard screaming from the cellar again, louder and more distinct than before. But this time, while it was definitely animalistic, it wasn't an animal. I pressed my ear to the door and this time, I identified the source. It was Tina. And she wasn't being butchered. I'd recognize that screaming orgasm anywhere by now. She certainly never came that hard with me. I felt a little humiliated, but too anxious to dwell on my insecurities. It was time to go.

At the bar for a farewell brunch with the gang, I asked Marietta about it. She seemed genuinely puzzled and said she knew nothing about any butcher, and Tina had never been married. All she knew was that Tina was a disgraced beauty queen turned vagrant hooker. While passing through town, she decided to stick around once an employment opportunity presented itself, moving into the mansion as a gift from the locals, turning tricks with absolute privacy since everyone else was afraid to go inside, except for cheap suckers offered free room and board, like me. Rumor had it a serial killer had once lived there, and it might be haunted, but that's all Marietta would tell me.

I was intrigued and knew she was at least partially lying but I let it go since I was on my way out the door anyway, and I didn't want to push my luck, which sometimes pushes back even harder. As Marietta reminded me, I had been free to leave at any time since I arrived. But I didn't, and having done her research, she knew damn well I wouldn't. Someone lost a bet.

Sensing my parting discomfort, Eryk folksily explained the whole point of this set-up while I was waiting for my cab to the airport. "Right now, each of us is writing the same story," he said with a loaded grin, "meaning this one, but with a different twist ending. We're reading it at our next gathering, called Noir at the Bar, which you'll miss, unfortunately."

"No. I won't miss it," I said, but he just talked right over me.

"Fortunately for you, *this* ending happens to be *your* ending. At least in real life."

"This time, anyway," I said, noticing for the first time the dark red stains on the floor beneath me. Maybe I was still being unreasonably paranoid, given the overall hospitality, but the substance seemed too thick and sticky to be vermouth. It also rang an alarm when I discerned that they were in the shape of footprints. Big footprints.

Just then Shawn came up behind me, startling me

with a slap on the shoulder. I nearly peed my pants.

"How was your stay with us, son?"

"Fleeting but fulfilling."

"That's more than most folks I meet down at the crematory could say."

"Huh?"

He let out a booming laugh, then slapped me on the shoulder again, even harder, knocking me off balance. Inadvertently, I assumed. "I meant *Life*, my man, relax! Not everyone gets what they came for. It's a short ride for everyone but not everyone enjoys it. Some more than others, so you're one of the lucky ones. Let's face it: *none* of us get out of here alive. So we might as well have some fun while we're here!"

"Oh," I said with a stupid, sheepish grin.

"That's why we're all here, I think," Eryk said.

"To have a good time?"

"To be put in an evolving variety of situations with infinite outcomes and choices, just to see what we'll do," Shawn said.

"Oh."

"Maybe we'll see you again sometime," Eryk said to me rather slyly when the cab arrived.

"Cheers," I said with a terse, noncommittal smile, which was my polite way of saying "fuck off and hell, no."

I ran to that goddamn cab and never looked back, except for a few fleeting glances over my shoulder.

Shortly after I got home, I read about a murder in that town that made national headlines for its horrific details. The victim was Tina. The first thing I thought was I could've saved her if I wasn't such a horny, selfish asshole. But then maybe not. My retconned impression was she was resigned to a gruesome death, too miserable to go on for reasons I didn't understand, and I was her final corporeal fling before eternal abstinence in the Big Nothing. Of course, this was more of a guilt-ridden rationalization than a logical theory. Nobody could want this, for any reason. She'd been found nude, ravaged, and dismembered in the woods, like the Southern Black Dahlia. Easier just to hang oneself.

I was plagued by the notion I had missed a lot of clues and details while lost in my fog of lust. But I'm always plagued by that notion since I'm always lost in a fog of lust, so I didn't let it bother me any more than usual.

The article mentioned she had once been a mystery writer, something she never told me, but then she didn't divulge much about her past, and I didn't care to ask since our relationship was built not to last. Anyway, I looked her up online and found one of her stories, which was poetically constructed, if also grimly hardboiled. It was set at the bar, and it was about a detective from San Francisco who winds up dead, butchered, and dumped in a swamp. So far there are no suspects. In either case.

The story, entitled "Living Proof," had been self-published on her obscure blog two years before my trip.

(Originally published in shorter form in *Dark Yonder: Tales & Tabs*, Joyride Press, 2019, substantially augmented and altered for this collection.)

SOFT OPENING

Seattle, 1982

Ray Xavier—better known as "X-Ray"—was putting up the spectacularly lurid one-sheet poster for the Seattle premiere of *Cocktopussy: Tentacle-Testicles of Terror* in the outside display case as his favorite new song "Escalator of Life" was blasting from the radio inside the lobby of the recently renovated and reopened theater, formerly an Art Deco palace called The Grand, now a porno-grindhouse called The Rabbit Hole. He then went inside to the tiny office and turned on the customized, pink, bunny-shaped neon sign above the marquee. Just then the ominous clouds began to weep, making the venue seem that much more cozy and inviting, especially for patrons who were planning on wearing raincoats, anyway. Life was good. But that was about to change drastically.

Next, Ray—a former burlesque emcee and bar bouncer, wearing his best vintage sharkskin suit, his black hair slicked back so he looked like a lounge lizard pimp, which wasn't far from the truth—ran up to the booth to check with Max, the pimply-faced young projectionist.

"How's the print?" Ray asked.

"It's almost brand new!" Max said enthusiastically. "So it's fine. I just finished building it up, in fact."

"I was worried since it's coming off a three-month run in Times Square," Ray said. "And frankly, the distribution company seems a little shady to me. I'm suspicious they're Mafia or something. So secretive and sleazy. We'll need to be careful about paying them, just to be safe, since I don't want to wind up at the bottom of Puget Sound due to delinquent bills. I was raised in New Jersey and I know the type, trust me."

"The Mob is infiltrating the porn racket big time, I hear," Max said. "That would be kinda cool though, right? To be in bed with real gangsters? As it were."

"You're totally romanticizing that milieu, kid. You don't want to mess around with those guys. I'm glad they didn't stick us with a totally trashed print, anyway, since this is our first night of business, however unofficial. First impressions count, especially when your main source of promotion is word of mouth."

"Well, my assessment of the print does come with a *caveet*."

"A *caveet*? What the hell is that, a side dish?"

"Huh?"

"You mean a *caveat*, you idiot."

"Don't call me an idiot. Insults are against union rules."

"Fuck the union. What are you trying to tell me, Max?"

"I can't promise the reels will be in order."

"What the hell are you talking about?"

"Well, they weren't numbered, so it was hard to tell. I tried checking to make sure the continuity was intact, but I won't know for sure until I run it once. If you let me do a trial screening, I could be sure."

Ray looked at his watch. "That's what happens

when they deliver the print the day the movie opens. Bastards. First show is in two hours. How long is this stupid fucking film, anyway?'

"Eighty-two minutes of non-stop fetishistic fornication, from what I can tell. So maybe it doesn't matter if the reels are out of order? It's not like anyone is paying any attention to the plot anyway, right? Still, I take pride in my work. It's my responsibility and I'd like to get it right so we don't completely embarrass ourselves on opening night in front of paying customers. Nobody wants to patronize amateurs. Not even scumbags and perverts."

"Okay, go ahead, but that's cutting it close, literally, since you may have to rearrange the reels before show time."

Max saluted Ray, then nodded and turned on the projector.

"Hey, can you bring me something to snack on?" Max asked. "I'm famished!"

"'Famished? Who the fuck says 'famished'!"

"Hungry people who own a thesaurus, which I can't eat."

"Free meals are not in the contract, but in the spirit of professional courtesy, at least tonight, hang on, I'll be right back," Ray said with mild irritation before Max ran downstairs and plopped down in one of the plush new seats.

Ray went back into the lobby where his business partner Hal was behind the concession stand making popcorn. Hal, a grizzled, gruff, fifty-five-year-old veteran of the film exhibition industry, asked Ray suddenly, "Did you ever throw up on someone while having sex?"

"No! That's disgusting! What am I, Charles Bukowski? Why even ask?"

"Just wondering if it's normal, that's all."

"Why, did you?"

"Maybe," Hal said with a shrug.

"Never mind this neurotic nonsense now. Can you bring Max a bag of that shit? He's watching the film now to make sure the fucking reels are in order like that even matters."

"Shit? It's not shit. Well, the popcorn isn't, I haven't seen the movie yet. It's totally fresh! You watched me just make it! Even the butter is real!"

"Well, it won't be fresh anymore when we actually open, moron. Why are you making it now?"

"I'm hungry! I can always make more. And don't call me a moron."

"Can you please not eat all our goddamn food before we actually sell any? You know concessions will be our main source of revenue. It's the only way we can compete with the goddamn video cassette tape market."

"Like people can't order pizza while jerking off on their own couch. We need to get a beer license, I'm telling you, or else this whole project is doomed."

"Hal, why did you even go into this venture with me if you're going to have that negative attitude?"

"Just being realistic, Ray. And reality sucks. Look around. Single-screen theaters like this are closing right and left. That's how we got *thi*s one, for a song, too."

"What song was that?"

"'I think it was 'Brother, Can You Spare a Dime.'"

"The Tom Jones version."

"Of course. Fuck Bing Crosby. Tom knows how to put the 'pain' in 'window pane.'"

"No, that lyric is from a totally different song, dumbass. 'I, Who Have Nothing.'"

"That's the one we'll both be singing tomorrow."

"Hal, you didn't answer my question. My first one."

"I grew up in this business, Ray. It's in my blood. You were also basically raised in my dad's theaters since your asshole parents were absent and movies were your babysitter, so it's in your blood, too. I told you we'd be better off with a repertory operation, with or without beer, but no, you had to play it dirty, pandering to the lowest common denominator. I admit sex sells, but people prefer privacy when it comes to this stuff, and with modern technology, they can have their boner and pull it, too, without worrying about getting arrested. Since you came up with most of the investment money, even if it was from selling hard drugs on the street, I went along. I'm just biding my time, though, till I'm proven right."

"Shit, Hal, even old movies are available in the home video market. Then there's cable TV. Next, they'll let you watch anything you want on a personal computer. I admit, you're probably right. The odds are against us no matter what we show. I just don't know what the hell else to do with my life. Maybe I just should go ahead and die."

"Ray, for Chrissake, lighten up, already. You're too pretty to die so young."

"That just means I'll leave a good-looking corpse. Only the pretty die young. Like Jim and Marilyn and Elvis."

"No, no, only the *good* die young."

"Right. It's the assholes who stick around and fuck everything up."

"Anyway, Ray, like I've been trying in vain to explain to you, classic movies are a communal experience, traditionally speaking. Porn doesn't need to be publicly exhibited to be appreciated. The less company the better, if you know what I mean. Unless it's a circle jerk. Which we won't allow, I trust. We'll try your way first, though, and if it doesn't work out, as it most likely won't, we'll adapt and experiment and grow over time, like any other independent business."

"Then suddenly fold without notice."

"Exactly. But at least we can delay the inevitable and have some fun in the meantime."

"Hal, c'mon. Concessions provide most of the profits regardless of the type of movies we show since those goddamn rental and shipping fees suck up most of our budget anyway. And we can't get a beer license just like that, it's not easy, especially since we show porn. Remember, sex and booze can't legally mix in this state, I mean as far as exhibition. Which goes back to your original point, granted. But unless and until you get to shove this all back in my face, please, I beg you, don't recklessly consume all our inventory so we can have a fighting chance at least before we resort to being just another legit cookie-cutter cop-out whore, please, huh?"

"We got plenty of everything food-wise, man. Popcorn, pretzels, hot dogs, candy, you name it. It'll be a veritable fuck-fest-feast. I'm more worried we won't have enough customers to justify it all. If we stocked beer as I've been strongly suggesting from the start, we could turn this place into a survivalist bunker if we had to, and with Reagan in charge now, a zombie apocalypse is right around the corner. We're all gonna die soon, anyway. Meantime, just relax." Hal grabbed a handful of popcorn and threw it at Ray. They started giggling like little boys, randomly reverting to their adolescent rapport.

"*You* relax, you swine-shit slurping, simian-semen-swilling *slob*," Ray said with mock disdain.

"Hey *fuck you,* you donkey dick-sucking monkey-whore!"

"Kiss my ass, you facile fecal fetishist!"

"Bend over and I'll jam my manly fist up your torn, bloody butthole, you babbling baboon *bitch*!"

"You need to be hog-tied, horse-whipped, and gang-raped doggy style by a maniacal mob of mutated maggots!"

"Yeah, while you wank on your little worm watching us, you pathetic puerile perverted *punk*!"

"Your juvenile gibberish and facile drivel have grown tiresome. Shut your pie hole and bring Max a bag of that crappy popcorn."

"Shut up."

"*You* shut up."

"Fuck you."

"Fuck *you.*"

"Am I interrupting anything, boys?" a silky feminine voice suddenly said from just inside the front door as lightning flashed and thunder boomed.

Ray and Hal turned to face the stranger. She was a breathtakingly beautiful blonde wearing Ray-Ban sunglasses and a long, shiny, black leather trench coat. Her long, lean, shapely legs led down to spiky, snakeskin pumps, and her copious cleavage practically popped out of its slick, sartorial confines, strongly suggesting she was completely nude beneath the coat. Her flawless complexion was like warm ivory.

"Who are you?" an instantly entranced Hal asked at the same time as an equally enthralled Ray said, "How can we help you?"

"Why, I'm here for the premiere of my film," the woman replied. "Don't you recognize me?"

She opened up the trench coat and fully exposed her impossibly curvaceous and indeed completely naked body.

"Maybe if you took off the shades," Hal said with a laugh.

"Wait a minute, you're Alicia Armstrong!" Ray exclaimed. "You're the main female love interest for the Cocktapus, right? Now I recognize you from the poster and press kit!"

"Holy shit!" Hal said. "I didn't know you were even invited! Why didn't you tell me, Ray!"

"I didn't invite her either!" Ray said. "Not that I wouldn't, I just didn't think any of the stars would come all the way to Seattle just for this."

"Well, frankly, I heard about the opening night in the paper, and since I'm from here, I thought I might as well show up," the luscious lady said. "This was my favorite theater growing up. In fact, I used to dance here when it was briefly a burlesque hall, back in the Sixties."

"But you don't look a day over…" Ray stopped himself for fear of being inadvertently rude. Alicia Armstrong only looked to be about twenty-five, meaning she'd been a professional exotic dancer at age five or so, by logically chronological calculations.

"Anyway, whatever or whoever brought you here, very glad to have you!" Ray went up to shake her hand, even as the sight of her perfect figure in all its glorious proximity overwhelmed his senses.

Alicia closed her coat and tied it shut before accepting Ray's gesture. "Thank you. And you are?"

"You can call me X-Ray," he said. "This here is Hal, my partner. Inside the theater is Max, our projectionist. He's checking on the print as we speak. Would you care to join the preview screening? We'd all be honored!"

"Sure," she said. "I haven't actually even seen it yet!"

"Neither have I!" Hal said, still leering at her longingly. "Though we heard good things. It has quite a reputation. That's why we chose it for our premiere."

"Where did you say you heard about us again?" Ray asked her as they headed inside the cavernous auditorium. "We actually didn't spring for any ads yet, relying on word of mouth until we work out the kinks, so to speak. This is basically a trial run."

"Yeah, I was wondering the same thing," Hal said.

"Word gets around the underground grapevine," Alicia said. "I just thought I'd surprise you."

"You sure did!" Hal said.

"I guess the distributor told you?" Ray suggested.

"Perhaps," she said with cryptic caution.

But the graphic celluloid distraction looming before them quickly derailed the conversation. Up on the big screen, Alicia's voluptuous visage was sucking voraciously on one of Cocktopus's massive tentacles, while another tentacle pleasured her gushing pussy and yet another was indelicately probing her juicy anus.

The practical effects were incredibly impressive for a low-budget exploitation production. For one thing, the monster didn't look like a man in a rubber suit. It looked like an actual monster. Of course, Alicia required no prosthetics to augment her visage. She was all real, as her surprise presence proved.

The Cocktopus, at least in the "script," was a horrible, horny alien monster that had come here to mate with female humans, since all the women of his planet had been wiped out in a mysterious plague. Each of the monster's eight limbs was actually a penis that could ejaculate buckets of semen all over the outside and inside of his sex partners. On-screen, Alicia's seven equally gorgeous "roommates" suddenly walked in on the sordid scene, and, impressed by both the power and number of orgasms being experienced and witnessed, immediately began disrobing, so the Cocktopus could fuck all of them at once. It was obviously the most outrageously explicit and ambitiously choreographed sequence in the history of the genre, and all three men were pleasantly dumbstruck. No one moved for several minutes, paralyzed and hypnotized by the astonishingly stimulating spectacle.

Finally sensing her compellingly charismatic presence behind him, Max suddenly turned around and immediately recognized Alicia as the feminine star of the mesmerizing movie. Since no one had bothered to formally introduce them, he shot up to greet her politely, then humbly sat back down, gaping at her lustfully in between glances back at her cinematic doppel-gang-banger.

"So didn't the guy inside the rubber suit get to

actually screw anyone?" Hal asked.

"What guy inside what suit?" she said, and they all laughed. Except for her.

"What is that sticky shit shooting out of him, anyway?" Ray said. "A mixture of milk and mayonnaise? Must've made you sick after a while, sucking and swallowing all that fake cum, not to mention wallowing in it."

"It wasn't fake," she said. "It was actually quite tasty. I couldn't get enough of it. None of us could. *Watch*."

The males all adjusted the crotches of their pants in attempts to either conceal or suppress their painful hard-ons as the bestial onscreen orgy intensified, with the "actresses" enjoying multiple successive orgasms as the Cocktopus showered them all with the icky liquid spraying from its eight limbs like uncontrolled fire hoses.

"The Japs are into this kinky shit," Hal said. "Plus rubber monster suits are their specialty. I wonder if those creepy cocksuckers financed this sick little flick. They really get their jollies watchin' whores, excuse me, *women* gettin' raped by animals 'n' shit. Any idea who the backers were, Ms. Armstrong?"

"This movie was funded by outside interests," she said as she continued watching with unnerving solemnity, her sunglasses still mysteriously in place on her coldly beautiful face. "There's no need to be racist. Or misogynistic. Or homophobic, for that matter. Your kind can be so petty."

Suddenly Ray, Hal, and Max grew very uncomfortable, shifting in their seats, and not just so they could adjust their leaking penises. Not wishing to cross any more invisible politically correct boundaries, feeling morally ambushed by this feminist freak, they all remained silent for the remainder of the screening.

Once Max went up to the booth and brought the house lights up, Ray and Hal stood up and stretched. Alicia remained seated, still very quiet and eerily contemplative.

"Well, I'm gonna get ready to let the folks in, if there are any," Ray said with a nervous chuckle. "Would you like to come greet our guests with me? It would give them quite an unexpected thrill."

"There won't be any guests," Alicia said without moving her head, or even her lips, it seemed. "Only unexpected thrills."

"What do you mean?" Hal asked with trepidation.

She didn't respond, maintaining her mannequin-like stillness.

"I have a more positive prediction!" Ray said with forced optimism. "We're gonna sell out the house! Even without the benefit of advance advertising! That marquee alone will attract drive-by traffic! We may even cause a few accidents, haha! Of course, that would've been easier if we could've promoted your appearance, but…"

Alicia smiled slyly and then slowly removed her Ray-Bans. Her glowing orbs had no pupils. She popped them out and discarded them like they were old mothballs. Next, she removed her blonde wig, followed by the synthetic skin on her phony skull helmet, which was also flung aside. Then she stood straight up and took off the trench coat along with the rest of her fabricated flesh, finally revealing her true identity: Cocktopus itself.

The men all screamed and tried to escape out the fire exit as the monster's wildly flailing tentacles lashed out and grabbed each one by the throat, strangling them into submission. Since there were only three victims, the Cocktopus had five free arms with which to tear off their clothes and savagely ravage their orifices, filling them to the brim with its organic seminal fluid until they all literally choked on it. Additionally, the sizzling substance was lethally acidic, burning the flesh from their very bones, while disintegrating their internal organs, which flushed out of their anal cavities like gory diarrhea. But their intense agony stopped abruptly when the monster tore their limbs and torsos apart in a carnally carnivorous frenzy.

Several of the monster's voyeuristic companions— discreetly watching the entire gruesome scenario gradually then suddenly unfold from the back of the theater—suddenly swarmed and devoured the remains of the men while one of the Cocktopi stood back and continued filming the festivities with an elaborate, portable alien camera.

A mile or so above The Rabbit Hole, a strange but sleekly stylish spaceship was hovering in the stormy skies, its occupants gleefully monitoring the mayhem via a massive console screen.

"'Cocktopussy 2: Movie Theater Massacre' will be our most successful porno snuff film yet," the eight-limbed director proudly proclaimed in its native tongue as the fully sated Cocktopi below left the theater just before a single blast from the spaceship set it ablaze, destroying any trace of what had transpired inside. "Especially in Japan."

"*Damn*!" said the corpulent, lonely man in a raincoat, staring forlornly at the raging inferno from across the street as fire engine sirens wailed in the distance. He had hoped to buy the first ticket. "Just my luck."

(Originally published in *Knucklehead Noir*, Coffin Hop Press, 2019.)

DESPERATE PERCEPTION

Capitol Hill, Seattle, 2025

With a start that leaves him momentarily breathless, The Lost Man wakes up from another dream right before the payoff. As in his waking life, he leaves a lot of unfinished business in his dreams. It's the daydream he always wakes into that worries him since its corporeal existence sustains these alternate, internal dimensions, and he's afraid that when he dies, his dreamworlds will fade away and disappear along with his consciousness. The Lost Man lives only for the freedom and comfort of his surrealistic subconscious, where he suspects his long-lost love may be hiding. When he has dream awareness, something he usually only enjoys while awake, he looks for her inside these nocturnal visions, even though he's no longer sure she ever existed on this side of reality's duplicitous veil.

If only he could stay focused on a single thought for more than a moment, The Lost Man might be able to figure out what's missing, or who's missing, but his mind wanders like a restless nomad in search of an oasis he knows is a mirage, but it's the only sanctuary that welcomes him. And it beats the finality of the ruthless alternative.

Recently, Death has been like a hitman with a personal vendetta against everyone and everything left in this world that he cherishes. David Lynch is dead. Tom Robbins is dead. Olivia Hussey is dead.

Democracy is dead. The A's left Oakland. His favorite bar The Jilted Siren with the mermaid motif suddenly shuttered. This world is filled with ghosts but has lost its spirit. In order to be happy, The Lost Man has to let go of his lifelong daydreams of happiness. They are spoiling whatever time he has left. Time passes quickly and is forgotten even quicker. Days melt into nights which freeze over and thaw by morning. He doesn't understand what that means even though he made it up himself.

The Lost Man likes where he lives, a small midcentury apartment in the Capitol Hill neighborhood of Seattle, functionally furnished. He especially likes that his apartment is right next door to the mailroom.

"I should live *in* the mailroom," he once told a fellow resident while loitering in the lobby. "It would be even more convenient. I wouldn't have to pay rent, and I would get my mail right away. I love surprise packages."

"What's a typical surprise package for you?" the neighbor asked, somewhat wary of him, like all the residents.

"Any package."

The only mail The Lost Man ever receives is the monthly disability checks. They've been his only source of financial sustenance for so long that he can't remember how or why he's disabled, so he always cashes them immediately in case the mysterious investors financing the movie of his existence realize that he isn't handicapped at all, it's all been a big mistake, and he has to pay it back. Unless it's the Mob. Then they'll just break his kneecaps and call it even.

All these checks but no balance.

The Lost Man can't relate to the modern world, and the world is always modern in the moment. He likes vintage movies from a particular period with a certain mood and aesthetic that reflects his 21st-century black-and-white mental oasis of crime jazz, shattered dreams, desperation, and depression. *The Hustler*. *Sweet Smell of Success*. *Too Late Blues*. *Blast of Silence*. *Night Tide*. *Daughter of Horror*. *I Was a Teenage Werewolf*. *Spider Baby*. Russ Meyer's *Lorna* and *Mudhoney*. Old TV detective shows like *Johnny Staccato* and *Honey West*. He also likes *The Outer Limits*, because he lives on the fringe.

Additionally, The Lost Man likes relatively contemporary movies that explore themes of Sex and Death via dreamlike aesthetics, like those of Gaspar Noé, such as *Irreversible* and *Enter the Void*. Yorgos Lanthimos' *Poor Things,* Robert Eggers' *Nosferatu,* and Andrzej Żuławski's more vintage classic *Possession* are among his favorite films. But for his money, and he is always broke, no one could touch David Lynch, even in death. No one can touch anyone dead, but the dead can still touch us, he once told himself. *Lost Highway* is his favorite David Lynch movie.

Currently, the Lost Man's overall favorite movie if he had to pick one which he doesn't is *Looking For Mr. Goodbar*. He finds its erotic nihilism mesmerizing, It's one reason he's single. Every time he shows it to whoever he is with, rewinding the shocking final scene over and over because it's so brilliantly disturbing he can't stop watching it, his female companion leaves. They always tell him on the way out the door that it was simply the final straw. His obsession with one of the most brutal murders in cinematic history, a fixation he claims is justified by its ingenious editing and artistic integrity, only confirms their worst fears about his emotional and psychological instability, which is not just fragile, but broken.

The Lost Man tries to be a good person and a good lover. But his dark side always overshadows his brightest efforts, which are half-hearted anyway, and the bad half is stronger than the good one.

"I'm happy when you're happy," The Lost Man once said to an old girlfriend. At least he thought she was his girlfriend.

"I'm never happy," she said.

"That's why I'm so depressed."

"You were already depressed."

"But you brought me out of it."

"I thought you said you were feeling my pain?"

"I've lost the distinction."

"Let me make it easy for you."

One day The Lost Man receives a notice from the landlord ordering him to stop bringing prostitutes back to his apartment or face immediate eviction, because the sounds of intermingling pain and pleasure emanating at late hours from his place were indistinguishable and disturbing the neighbors. He was confused because he hadn't paid for sex in years, not since his last girlfriend left him. Or at least it felt like years. Sometimes, though, it felt like only yesterday. Maybe it was. The Lost Man has no sense of Time anymore. He doesn't miss it. It's only trying to kill him, anyway.

Different things beyond his control dictate his

mood. Politics. The weather. Bowel movements. The Lost Man never finished high school and once even cheated on a poop test. Instead of sampling his own excrement to mail back to the hospital for a colon cancer screening, he went to a public bathroom and waited for a little kid to take a dump, then burst into the stall and scared him before the kid could even flush. The kid ran out crying with his pants around his ankles. This stolen shit sample would statistically be free of any disease. If he was dying, he didn't want to know. That would ruin the surprise.

Someone is looking out for him and always has been, or so The Lost Man chooses to believe since he is otherwise all alone in the Universe. Plus he doesn't understand why else he continues to endure such a solitary existence, even if he convinces himself his isolation from society is voluntary. Living in various residential hotels, and briefly on the streets, The Lost Man has encountered and survived many violent brushes with Death, not to mention starvation and exposure to the elements.

Now he has a nice little pad equipped with his basic necessities, meaning a bed, a radio, a TV, an old but functional Blu-Ray player with a small collection of his favorite movies, and an old record player with some of his favorite LPs, all afforded on his unwarranted disability income, except for the stolen items which are most of them. Plus a rich man's view of the Space Needle, a daily gift beyond his social worth as a human being. The Lost Man assumes his Guardian Angel is God, or better yet, Goddess, in the holy visage of Hammer horror film actress Valerie Leon.

He is grateful for his newly earned senior discount

at the movies. Age brings a belated appreciation of the mundane, infusing even the most mundane details with urgent preciousness.

The Lost Man doesn't understand his own species and tries to avoid them, which is easy since it's a case of mutual apathy. He spends most of his time alone in his apartment, staring at the TV or into space, listening to jazz, and asking himself rhetorical questions, such as:

"When people say 'it was meant to be,' they only mean good things. Why not bad?"

"Other than aesthetics, what's the difference between a psycho serial killer wearing a corpse's face and someone wearing a fur coat?"

Like Dexter at a homicide scene, the serial killer of serial killers masquerading as a forensic blood spatter analyst, guilty of the same sorts of crimes he is investigating, The Lost Man once gave Life a spot analysis and came up with no evidence, not even proof of life. He hasn't tried again since. Like the poop test, he doesn't want to know the truth.

The Lost Man likes to sit in cafes and read books, which no one but him does anymore. His favorite author at the moment is James Ellroy because the prose style is succinct yet poetic and his midcentury milieu is brutal yet stylish. So many ugly people in a world of beauty. Plus they both lost their mothers to homicidal tragedies, which has haunted them both for life. The Lost Man's mother, who raised her only child as a single parent, was mentally ill and abusive towards him until he was taken away by Child Protection Services and placed in various foster homes until he finally ran away and disappeared. His mother was found raped and murdered while living on the streets, according to court filings that he keeps in a tattered envelope under his bed, the only clues he has to his former life, though most of the pages are missing. The Lost Man has no memories or pictures of his mother but imagines her resembling Diane Keaton. He thinks he's inherited her damaged genes. At least he has someone dead to blame it on.

The Lost Man wonders while washing his hands why water has to be so wet because he can't seem to get them completely dry.

He enjoys wandering all over Capitol Hill and downtown Seattle. He aimlessly walks so much that he develops a sharp, twisting pain in his right knee that tingles and radiates up and down his leg, making him hobble as it buckles beneath the pressure. Then he starts violently coughing and sneezing and has trouble breathing. As usual, The Lost Man fears the worst and is always disappointed.

An old lady—older than him—in the lobby of his building scolds him for not wearing a mask in the lobby.

"Why should I?"

"Maybe it's Covid."

"I doubt it. I haven't been close enough to anyone recently to catch it. Except you."

"What about the hookers?"

"What hookers?"

"I've seen them, you can't fool me. Maybe you got AIDS."

"They still get AIDS?"

"Who's 'they'?"

"Anyone."

"I don't know."

"Okay, shut up then."

The Lost Man goes inside his apartment and opens his stolen iPad, Googling the connection between a sudden cold with shortness of breath and a sore knee. Every WebMD bullshit reason from diabetes to cancer to a Government conspiracy pops up, and his paranoia keeps him awake all night. So he goes for a walk and gets mugged. The two thugs take the rest of the cash from his last disability check after they knock him down and kick him in the stomach. The Lost Man doesn't mind. The way he sees it, he deserves much worse, for reasons he can't quite place. He's getting off easy again.

The Lost Man can't seem to focus on any one subject for any length of time. One of his girlfriends told him he had ADD. He started to Google it but was distracted by a short video on a Celebrity Porn site of Barbara Crampton in *Body Double* which he repeated dozens of times so he never got around to his original search. Instead, he found her infamous scene from *Re-Animator* and watched that for the rest of the day.

Besides *Looking for Mr. Goodbar,* The Lost Man is obsessed with the 1966 film *Incubus*, starring William Shatner, the only movie ever made in the language of Esperanto. But he tries hard to ignore the subtitles so he can figure out the dialogue on his own, in the context of the situation. The Lost Man's goal is to learn the language of Esperanto, which would retcon the reason why it is so difficult for him to communicate with normal people. So far, it's not going well.

The Lost Man's favorite song, at least currently, is "Ain't No Sunshine When She's Gone," by Bill

Withers. All of his girlfriends were now gone, never to be seen or heard from again, not even by their few mutual friends, whom he lost once he lost the girls. Despite its melancholy refrain, or because of it, this song consoles him, since in Seattle, there was hardly any sunshine when his girlfriends were still here, anyway. He also likes the song "Death" by White Lies. He likes the band Pink Martini, at least their versions of "Bolero" and "Brazil" which he often plays in loops. His favorite band, though, is The Cramps.

One day while walking through an alley in his neighborhood The Lost Man is immediately enthralled by a green cellar door behind an old brick building. There's nothing particularly unique about it, other than the incidental urban poetry, a la Edward Hopper. However, if he stares at it long enough, he can imagine Leatherface suddenly opening the door, dragging someone inside, and slamming it. Unfortunately, real life isn't as exciting as movies. Or dreams.

The Cramp's version of "Green Door" springs to mind as he continues staring into the crevices and cracks beneath the green paint, which contain secrets. Something about the green door intrigues him, and he is curious about where it leads, even if it's a basement. He is compelled to enter but fights the temptation when consumed by a powerful dread. The seduction of the forbidden haunts him as he forces himself to keep walking.

To soothe his nerves and consider his options, The Lost Man goes to Donna's to enjoy his usual plate of pasta, followed by a Mai Tai around the corner at the tiki karaoke bar Hula Hula, topped off with a nightcap across the street from there at the 1960s LP themed=bar Revolver, followed by a slice of pizza at Dino's up the block. He doesn't talk to anyone and no one talks to him. It's as if he doesn't even exist. But the pain in his heart reaffirms his relative reality.

Back home The Lost Man watches all eighteen episodes of *Twin Peaks: The Return* in bed so he can take quick naps, then wake up and rewind, his bedside table equipped with junk food, booze, and bottles of prescription pills he has never taken, the bathroom only steps away. This is how he wants to spend eternity, and he prays nightly for it to be so.

Finally, he falls into a deep slumber just as Kyle MacLachlan yells, *"What year is this?"*

The next morning, The Lost Man has his usual morning cup of damn fine coffee in his RR cup from Twede's Cafe in nearby North Bend (though he thought he had only dreamed being there since he has no car), then he goes outside and knocks on the green door. The morning is strangely still and quiet, with no one around, not even birds. He keeps knocking. No answer. Then he notices the green door is slightly ajar, so he pushes it open, and tentatively steps inside the foreboding darkness.

A light goes on inside his head, illuminating his location.

Beyond the green door, he gradually recognizes his own bedroom in his own apartment, but it's been reinterpreted as an Expressionistic set from an old favorite of his, *The Cabinet of Dr. Caligari*. Confused, he turns around and panics when he sees there's no exit, not even a door to the living room. The window with the spectacular view of the Space Needle is still there, but it's no longer a glass portal; it's simply replicated as an Impressionistic painting on a solid wall. It feels too real to be a dream, but just in case it is, he does what he always does when he has dream awareness and he isn't comfortable with the current situation: he tries forcing himself to wake up.

But he doesn't. Because that alternate realm, the one he was escaping when he slept, has been closed to him, seemingly forever. The Lost Man suddenly remembers his disability.

Eraserhead is playing on the TV, but he can't find the remote, so he will never be able to turn it off or change the channel. Though this movie would be among his Desert Island choices, that decision was made when such a fantasy scenario was safely impossible, making it easy to pick. The Lost Man is nauseatingly aware of the inevitable banality of repetition, deeply concerned about the eternal lack of options. Worse, "Green Door" by The Cramps is playing in a continuous loop from an unknown source, sonically conflicting with the TV, but he is unable to control the volume of either and quickly decides it's his least favorite Cramps song. Then it just gets louder.

The Lost Man notices only one book in the room—an obscure pornographic novel by Ed Wood called *The Only House*—which is on his bedside table next to a bottle of whiskey. He will need that to read the book.

Then as his eyes scan away from the bedside table, The Lost Man beholds a breathing, breathtaking visage of Valerie Leon as she appeared in *Blood from the Mummy's Tomb,* lying naked on his bed, her eyes cold and lifeless but her warm body covered in blood, forever sentient but silent, able to provide endless sensual pleasure but no true companionship, frozen in a state of suspended cinematic animation.

The room goes pitch black, and the relatively normal lighting is replaced with strobe light effects, like the ending of *Looking for Mr. Goodbar*. Valerie Leon, who always reminded him of his missing, dead, or fantasy wife, is still motionless on the bed, but babbling in the language of Esperanto, which he cannot fully understand, though he roughly interprets some of her words as "get help," "stop," "no," "please," and "not your fault."

Afraid to touch her for fear of reenacting his favorite movie scene, The Lost Man decides to masturbate instead, but when he reaches down, he finds he has no penis. The voluptuous visage of Valerie is now making passionate love with the slimy demon monster from *Possession*, except after The Lost Man blinks a few times to clear his vision which is disturbed by the strobe lights, she looks like Isabelle Adjani, her incessant orgasms fueling his frustrated lust and tormenting his thwarted libido.

Suddenly he has the urge to pee.

Through the harsh lightning-like flashes, he sees the door to his bathroom has opened, and his penis has magically reemerged, so while Isabelle continues fucking the monster, he goes to relieve himself, the pleasure of release making him close his crying eyes, the tears dripping with toxicity like the mixture of urine and semen merging into a single flow down the drain.

The Lost Man pees for what seems like hours, and as he does, he travels deeper inward and remembers the night his wife was hit by a "confused" driver while she was walking home from a neighbor's house, where she was having an affair with a bodybuilder she met at the gym. The drunk driver was her husband, meaning The Lost Man, blinded by jealousy. Even though it was ruled an accident, and his sentence for vehicular manslaughter reduced to negligence, The Lost Man always blamed her death on her musclebound lover for taking her away from him, for turning her against him, for giving her a reason to walk home alone late at night when anything could happen, and finally did.

Years later, many years, years overflowing with emptiness, The Lost Man still isn't sure if it was intentional, because he knew killing her was the same as killing himself and he only wanted to die once her infidelity was confirmed. Then when she died, he was afraid of Death, because at least he could remember her while he remained alive.

The Lost Man knew before he killed her that he was pushing her away with his manic neuroses. It didn't matter that she pleaded with him to get help with his delusions which were becoming increasingly dangerous, along with the blackouts, the memory losses, the fits of frustration about being a failure with everything in his life but his marriage, and now that was failing, too.

It didn't matter she had been the only woman, or person, who ever loved him, who accepted him as he was, until his true nature revealed itself against his will since he couldn't control it, and it became unbearable for both of them. It didn't matter that she told him she loved him but couldn't live like this anymore. It didn't matter she promised never to leave but needed something—and ultimately someone—for herself, to maintain her own sanity, her own sense of self. None of it mattered anymore, and it never did.

That's when The Lost Man went on a killing spree, murdering prostitutes who reminded him of his wife, pretending they were his girlfriends, showing each of them *Looking for Mister Goodbar, w*hich had been his wife's favorite movie since it reminded her of how she might've ended up had she not met her husband. The rough sex he imagined he had with these hired women was healing and cathartic or might've been if he had actually fucked any of them. But he only paid them for their time, two and a half celibate hours, just to watch this one movie with him, quietly lying on his bed in his apartment, always turning up the volume of the final scene so everyone in the building could hear the self-abusive violence he felt churning inside of him day and night. Then the prostitute would leave with a chunk of his disability check, safe and sound if deeply saddened by the lonely man slowly dying of guilt and rage.

Suddenly he has lost any recollection of killing them.

For what seems like hours, The Lost Man is making love on top of a cold grave with Anna Falchi in *Cemetery Man*, but then her zombie lovers all rise from the dead at once and tear them both apart, meaning they pull her away from him, then actually tear him apart while he watches her being rapturously ravaged by rotting, ravenous sentient corpses as he lies helpless and dying, dismembered, merely a torso without any limbs or appendages, soon to be one of her undead suitors, though even then he won't be able to move, just roll around and bleed and drool while his true love is pleasured by his fellow ghouls.

The Lost Man opens his eyes and stares into the

bathroom mirror at the hideous reflection of his rotting face. Not wishing to believe it is true, he closes his eyes again as he continues to deliriously piss out his ecstatic orgasms in cathartic spurts.

Finally, the last bit of sperm-infused urine leaks out of the tip of his shriveled penis as he shakes it dry, then he wipes his sticky hands on his putrid face. The revelatory moments of clarity exposed by this cleansing of bodily fluids had passed—again—and his self-induced, selective amnesia, which he clings to so he can live long enough to properly mourn her, to wallow in his self-loathing, has returned. The Lost Man feels like himself again, a machinist who collects mementos, except for the sudden pain in his belly.

When The Lost Man opens his eyes again, he is standing stark naked outside the green door, safely back in his waking life and normal routine, or so he assumes since he can hear the birds, although they sound like they're in Hitchcockian distress. People are gathered around him, staring, pointing, and judging. He stands there staring at the green door with the knife in his hand, covered in blood that pours from an open wound in his stomach. A siren wails in the near distance, but that's not unusual in this neighborhood.

The Lost Man sees only one escape, and heads back through the green door, disappearing into the dark dream, merging with the madness, where she will live forever, be his forever, even if he has to share her with monsters because he is one himself, and he will never feel alone again…

The bright beams sporadically shooting around his head like faulty flashlights snap the driver of the old car out of his stupor just in time for him to slam on the brakes and skid off the icy pavement into a telephone pole. The woman crossing the street runs over to see if he's all right. Though his head hit the steering wheel and his forehead is bleeding, he looks up through blurred vision to behold the angelic visage of Valerie Leon, even though she is only a stranger who lives in the neighborhood. Or at least, he doesn't recognize her as anyone other than Valerie Leon.

"There really is a Goddess," he says before he passes out. She helps him out of the car and up to her apartment nearby. She distrusts doctors ever since a psychiatrist raped her in his office, so she crudely nurses him back to health, inexpertly and ultimately deficient due to her lack of medical knowledge, cuddling on her plush couch with him as they watch innocuous, romantic old movies like *Pillow Talk, Guys and Dolls,* and *The Girl Can't Help It*, even though he prefers horror movies as far as he knows. Without a history of experiences to inform him, his responses are all visceral.

When he finally awakens, he can't remember anything or anyone before the accident, except for movies he's seen, as if he lived them, though he feels like he knows his savior from somewhere in his past or future. She tells him that he's known her forever. He wishes he could remember, but he's glad he knows her now.

They fall in love and get married. Sometimes they fight, more often they fuck, sometimes both at once. They vow never to separate, regardless of space, time, reality, and dreams. Their mutual dread of loneliness continues to reunite them because no one else fills their void. As it were.

For now, they live together in a black-and-white movie with a low budget, so it has only brief flashes of lurid color. The score is all crime jazz.

Time is fluid, sometimes dripping like a torture technique, sometimes flowing in a disorienting torrent.

"I can't tell if my memories are dreams or my dreams are memories," he tells her.

"They're both intangible from this vantage point, so it doesn't matter."

"I had a dream I was old."

"You are old. You were young when we met last week."

"Shit. In most of my dreams, I'm still young. Like you are now. Forever young and beautiful, like when we first met so many years ago."

"But I'm old, too."

"Then you're ageless. Like a beautiful vampire."

"You mean a beautiful mummy."

"I do?"

"Trust me."

"I have no one else to trust," he says, "so I will."

"You're just seeing what you want to see when you look at me."

"I wouldn't change anything I see when I look at you."

"Because you already have. Many times."

"You changed for me?"

"I changed outwardly because it's our nature. I'm a different person now than when we met. I'll be different when we meet again. But only externally."

"Who are you now?"

"Whoever you need me to be to get through this evolving mirage."

"I need you to be mine."

"I'll never be yours, because no one belongs to anybody. We belong to the Cosmos. But I'll always be here when you need me, in one form or another."

"I want you to be the same forever, just as you are right now, even if everything else changes."

"Everything in this world constantly changes," she says. "It's called evolution."

"I'm resisting change. It's called revolution. Which are meant to bring change. No wonder it's not working."

"Revolutions also bring revelations."

"It's a revolving cycle."

"Only if you remember everything that came before. Otherwise, it always feels new."

"So I'm choosing to forget?"

"Your memory or rather your consciousness is selectively survivalist."

"I'm so confused."

"That means you're paying attention."

"Nothing makes any sense anymore."

"Nothing has to make sense as long as it's about something."

"So what is it all about?"

"You tell me."

"But I'm the one who asked the question."

"But you're the only one who can answer it."

"That doesn't make any sense."

"You're trying too hard to fathom the unfathomable. Live in the moment, one at a time."

"Eventually I'll die in one."

"For a moment."

"I'm afraid to enjoy anything because once I do, it

vanishes."

"Everything is a temporarily tactile illusion."

"I don't understand."

"This moment, you and me, this room, may not even be happening right now, or maybe it is happening, but not for the first time."

"As long as it isn't for the last."

"Nothing lasts forever, but everything repeats."

"You mean nothing is the only thing that lasts."

"Essentially, though nothingness is a meditative state of mind."

"I'm afraid of being nothing, living in nothing, because then I would be alone again."

"I promise never to leave you. Even if it's only in your dreams."

"I can always find you there?"

"Yes. If you remember me."

"How could I ever forget you?"

"The same way you forget everything else, except for movies."

"Movies aren't even real."

"They are to you, and that's all that matters. From your perspective, which is often in soft focus."

"I'm afraid if I can no longer see you I will forget what you look like, because then how can I find you?"

"Think of me right now as a movie, because you'll always have the video as a reference."

"Movies are only reflections of reality. I just can't always remember what they're reflecting."

"Because you want life to be a movie."

"Why?"

"You know why."

"Because of what happened a long time ago."

"Yes."

"I don't even remember what it was, only that it was something horrible because I can still feel it."

"It was horrible."

"I know I didn't mean it because I feel so bad about it."

"I know."

"It's terrible having remorse for something you can never recall."

"That's your punishment."

"I wish I could take it back."

"You can't. There's no taping over the past."

"But I can still feel the past."

"Then stop rewinding."

"Was I always like this? Even before the incident? I don't remember ever living like other people do."

"I don't know, since that was before I met you, even though we've known each other forever. My guess based on our eternal bond is it's a survival mechanism brought on by childhood trauma you don't know how to process in conventional terms."

"But what if I'm misremembering things I associate with movies?"

"You probably are."

"For instance, you look like that actress in that movie I showed you."

"Only to you."

"I can't help it. Movies last, life doesn't."

"Then think of me as her, and you will never forget me."

"Are you really here now, or is it a dream?"

"Reality is a dream. So yes."

"Then dreams are reality."

"Yes."

"That's contradictory. What's the distinction?"

"Perception."

"So you mean contraception."

"I mean anything you need me to mean so we can stop talking and fuck."

"I need you to mean what you say."

"I say what I mean."

"That's mean."

"It's all a means to an end, except it never ends."

"Then there's no escape, no exit from this nightmare."

"Never. Because you don't really want to escape, because there's no place else to go because nowhere else exists except the places you imagine."

"What if I don't imagine anything?"

"Then you're dead and it's too late."

"That's what I fear the most."

"I know."

"It feels like I've died many times, but I keep coming back to find you in my dreams. I can't dream if I'm dead."

"Death is one long dream. That's where you'll always find me, even if you don't remember my true face, because I'll be looking for you, too, and I'll never forget it."

He then tells her of a terrible recurring dream he has of her death when he ran into her that fateful night, literally. It's like an alternate reality. She tells him she has the same recurring dream of an alternate reality, only he was the one who died.

"Which dream is true?" he asks her.

"Whichever one we choose to believe," she says.

"I don't choose either."

"Life is filled with choices that are not of our choosing."

"That's heavy."

"Truth weighs on you."

"Let's forget it."

"If we remember to."

"I'm already starting to forget."

"Forget what?"

"I can't remember."

"Anytime you're confronted with reality, you replace it with a fantasy."

"Who will remember me? Who will tell my story?"

"I will. That's why I'm here. That's why I'm always here."

"But who will listen to my story?"

"Nobody."

"It feels like I don't even exist outside of my own imagination. And neither do you."

"It's a lot like that."

"Wait, I did remember something, or maybe it's a premonition. Were you the one sending me checks?"

"Only reality checks."

"I don't want to talk anymore," he says in a trance-like monotone.

"What would you like to do next?"

He thinks about it, then answers reflexively, "Want to watch a movie?"

"Sure," she says. "But this time, I'll choose."